THE
WOMAN NEXT DOOR

"Is something wrong, Marilyn?"

Marilyn saw the concern in Christine's eyes. But mixed with concern were determination, resolve—and pain.

"I like to think we're friends," Christine said anxiously.

"Nothing's wrong," Marilyn said. "I'd tell you if there was——" Suddenly Marilyn looked sharply to the left, toward the stairs. Was that a scream?

Christine went on chatting. How could she not have heard it? Marilyn was bewildered, confused. She looked toward the stairs again, waiting for the scream to be repeated.

**How could
Christine not hear
the thing that was
screaming in the attic?**

THE
WOMAN
NEXT
DOOR

T.M. WRIGHT

PLAYBOY
PAPERBACKS

Corn Hill is an actual preservation district in Rochester, New York. All other aspects of this work are fiction.

THE WOMAN NEXT DOOR

Copyright © 1981 by T. M. Wright

Cover illustration copyright © 1981 by PEI Books, Inc.

Published simultaneously in the United States and Canada by Playboy Paperbacks, New York, New York. Printed in the United States of America. Library of Congress Catalog Card Number: 81-47270. First edition.

Books are available at quantity discounts for promotional and industrial use. For further information, write to Premium Sales, Playboy Paperbacks, 1633 Broadway, New York, New York 10019.

ISBN: 0-872-16912-X (U.S.)
      0-872-16969-3 (Canada)

First printing October 1981.

Acknowledgments

I would like to thank Pat LoBrutto, Joanie Hitzig, and Fredrick Armstrong for their invaluable assistance in the preparation of this novel. Later thanks also to Bill Basile Jr.

For Mary Jane Basile and William G. Thompson

Prologue

After many minutes, the baby-sitter turned the TV down; it was ruining her concentration. She glanced at the telephone on the small white table just inside the entrance to the kitchen.

Later, she thought.

She crossed the living room, pushed the child's door open, and stood quietly, her eyes on the child. Finally, she reached around the right side of the doorway and flicked the light switch off.

She turned, went to the couch, sat and drummed her fingers—1-2-3-4—methodically on the armrest. She became aware of the fluid ticking of the grandfather clock near the front door. She glanced at it and grimaced. "Damn it!" she whispered.

One thing was certain: Six months of dull Friday nights shouldn't have ended like this. There was no reason for it to have come to this. Well, her own stupidity was the reason, wasn't it? Her own colossal stupidity. She grinned. *Colossal. Colossal stupidity.* She stopped drumming her fingers. *Colossal stupidity!* She'd use that phrase on some of the kids at school— Joanne Vanderburg, for one. "You're so colossally stupid!" she'd say. And then she'd walk off, leaving Joanne Vanderburg with her mouth wide open and with nothing to say. It was a nice thought.

Her grin vanished abruptly.

9

Now.

She stood, went to the telephone, picked up the receiver, dialed.

"Hello?" she heard.

"Is Mrs. Winter there, please?" she said.

"May I ask who's calling?"

"Her baby-sitter. This is her baby-sitter."

"Just a moment."

She heard, as if from a distance, "Evelyn, it's for you. Your baby-sitter."

She waited. Then: "Yes . . . this is Mrs. Winter."

"Mrs. Winter?"

"What is it? Is something wrong?"

"I don't know, Mrs. Winter." The baby-sitter paused briefly. "I mean . . . it's the baby——"

"The baby? What's happened to the baby?"

"Nothing. I mean . . . I don't know. She's so quiet. I think you'd better come home, Mrs. Winter."

"Quiet? What do you mean *quiet?*"

"Well, I mean she's breathing and everything, but . . . she's not moving. She fell. Out of her crib. She fell."

A short silence.

"Mrs. Winter?"

Then, again as if from a distance: "Oh, Jesus!" And a click, a dial tone.

The baby-sitter put the receiver on its rest. She went back to the child's room, turned the light on.

She saw that the child was almost exactly as she had left her—on her side at the back of the crib—except now her huge, impossibly blue eyes were open.

The baby-sitter glanced around the room, her face expressionless. Yes, everything was in order. She reached for the light switch. She hesitated. *The crib!* she realized. *The damned crib!*

She crossed to it, put her foot on the small pedal beneath and unlatched the left-hand side. She pushed down. The side gave a few inches. She stepped away.

Her gaze settled on the child.

She saw that the child was staring at her. Hard. Not with a bubbling smile ready on her lips, as if the baby-sitter were merely an object of amusement or curiosity, but hard. And cold. In emotion so intense that the muscles of the child's face had frozen, and all the energy in her small, quiet body had massed in the eyes.

Two weeks later

The baby-sitter got comfortable on the big couch. Well, it was too bad, she thought. Really too bad. Almost enough to make you cry, if you were used to crying, if it made you feel more human, if it "salved your conscience" (a phrase she had heard the day before, in English class, and thought was a very interesting phrase). She remembered crying—at the hospital, in the waiting room, while the doctors were busy finding out what had happened to the child (not what had been *done* to her, but what had *happened* to her). She had cried right in front of Mr. and Mrs. Winter.

("I'm sorry, Mrs. Winter, Mr. Winter. I'm so sorry. I should have——"

"It's okay, it's not your fault, not really.")

It had been just the right kind of weeping—good, dry, hesitant, confused. She'd kept it up, too, right up till the moment the doctor finally came into the waiting room.

("This is extremely difficult for me, Mrs. Winter——"

"My God, my baby is dead, my baby is——"

"No, Mrs. Winter, she's not dead. She has sustained some spinal injuries.")

And that—the baby-sitter readjusted herself on the couch—really was too bad, wasn't it? That was . . . tragic. Terrible. But accidents happened every day. No one was really to blame for them. They happened and that was that. It was fate.

The baby-sitter called, "Sammy, I thought I told you to stay the hell in your room," and got up from the couch; she was certain that little Sammy Watson, her latest charge (God, but wouldn't it be great if she didn't need to freakin' *baby-sit*, if she could just marry some guy who had a lot of money and he could set her up in some great big house and maybe she'd have a kid of her *own*), had gotten up again for another goddamned "dinkawawa." The baby-sitter turned and faced the stairway.

And very spontaneously peed in her pants.

Because the child on the stairs was not little Sammy Watson. But this child could not possibly *be* on the stairs, because she was five miles away in a hospital bed and she was all trussed up because she had "sustained some spinal injuries" because accidents happened every day, no one was really to blame, it was fate.

The baby-sitter mumbled something, her throat suddenly too dry for speech.

The child on the stairs grinned a big, wide, malevolent grin that made the baby-sitter wet her pants once more.

And then the child vanished.

The nurse's name was Simpson, and one word—*pathetic*—was going through her head now. Ever since the Winter child was brought in, two weeks before, that word had been running around inside Nurse Simpson's head. It was the only word that fit. And now it fit doubly well.

The nurse reached out and gently touched the sleeping child's lips. "I hope," she whispered—she felt a tear start—"that your dreams are good dreams, little one." She took her hand away. "And I hope you always have reason to smile."

Part One

BRETT

Chapter 1

1981

Christine Bennet knew that the whole thing would end in an argument, their first. And it was an argument that couldn't be avoided; that was the hell of it. His role, his position, as her husband, provider, a maker of decisions, and, yes, even her protector was at stake, regardless of how vehemently he'd deny it. And that all added up to a matter of pride. Better to injure him physically than to injure his pride.

"It's amazing, isn't it?" Tim Bennet said.

Christine nodded.

"A chance like this," he continued, "doesn't come along very often."

If only he wasn't so wildly enthusiastic, it would be easy to tell him, *Yes, Tim, you're right. But it just doesn't appeal to me. You understand, don't you?* And that would be the end of it and they could go on looking.

"In five years," Tim said, "this will be *the* place to live. Hell, it already is. Do you know that fifteen, twenty years ago you couldn't even drive through this area, let alone live here?"

"Uh-huh," Christine said.

"It's really amazing," Tim repeated.

Christine tried to fault him for his enthusiasm, his pride, tried to ascribe it to some lack of understanding, some break in communication that originated with him. But it was no good. He was what he was and she was what she was, and if he saw only so far, saw only what was apparent, it was because at this point in their marriage it was all he could deal with. A person learns to walk before he runs. Christine grinned at the cliché.

"What's funny?" Tim asked.

She looked at him. He was driving with both hands on the wheel, even though he was keeping the car just below the thirty-mile-an-hour limit. It was another sign of his protectiveness.

"Funny?" she said.

"You were smiling."

She thought a moment. "I was, wasn't I." She paused. "I don't remember why. Sorry."

He brought the car to a slow, easy stop at a red light. "See that house there?"

Christine looked. He had indicated a large, square, whitewashed brick building with a red stone roof and a small, nonfunctional wrought-iron porch under each of three front windows. The double front doors were of glass and oak; an oversized number *1* had been painted in yellow on the left-hand glass panel, and the number *4* on the other. The small, bright-green lawn was bordered by a tall, ornate fence, also of wrought iron. Christine thought the house forbidding and pretentious.

"Yes," she said.

"That was the first," Tim explained. "A man named Williamson bought it for fifteen hundred back around nineteen sixty-two."

"Fifteen hundred? Is *that* all?"

"It needed a lot of work, of course." The light changed. He pressed the accelerator gently. "I don't know exactly how much he had to invest to make it livable, but it was something like thirty thousand. And he had to do all the work himself, but that saved him a bundle. The house is worth at least a hundred thousand now."

"Sounds pretty impressive," Christine said, just missing the tone of enthusiasm she had tried for.

"Oh, it is, and that's why so many people latched on to the idea, and why there are so few houses left." He paused. "Light me a cigarette, would you, darling?" He pulled a pack of Marlboros out of his shirt pocket and handed it to her.

He parked the car in front of a big, rambling brownstone house. The windows on its first floor had been boarded over with plywood; most of its second-floor windows were broken; faded obscenities were visible on the sidewalk leading to the front door and on the door itself; there were gaping jagged holes scattered around the roof. Paradoxically, the lawn had recently been mowed, and the honeysuckle hedges encircling the house neatly trimmed.

Tim, leaning over, looking at the house through the passenger window, said, "That would cost us two thousand."

"Two thousand," Christine said, not as a question but merely for something to say. "It's certainly big, isn't it."

"Yes, it is."

"Be hell to heat."

"Absolutely."

"Are you thinking of buying it, Tim?"

He straightened, put the car in gear, and pulled slowly away from the house. "Hell no," he said. "It needs too much work. I've been through it. And besides, it's too big for just the two of us."

Christine thought she heard something vaguely accusatory in the way he said "just the two of us," but decided to disregard it. That delicate subject had yet to be opened, and it deserved far more attention than they could give it now.

*   *   *

Tim and Christine Bennet had been married for six months. The marriage was a culmination of a long and progressively more passionate relationship, the kind destined to make them husband and wife.

It was at first an uneasy relationship, one tinged by uncertainty. Because Christine, for nineteen of her twenty-one years, had been paralyzed from the waist down. All indications were that the paralysis was permanent. The wheelchair was her almost constant companion, and, predictably, it had drawn to her a succession of altruists, and men with pity to spread around and be known by, and, pathetically, the occasional oddball. But she learned quickly enough to identify each type and to cultivate a cool but polite attitude toward them.

When Tim came into her life, toward the end of her freshman year at Brockport State College—where she majored in fine arts and where he had a part-time position as an assistant professor of photography—she found that he was persistent, despite the attitude she cultivated. It became obvious that he saw through the façade, saw through to the spark of interest he had started in her. And he was so beautifully direct:

"You think I'm something other than what I appear to be, don't you, Christine?"

They were having lunch together on the college grounds. He hadn't asked the question offhandedly, eyes averted, in a foolish attempt to appear unconcerned, or subtle.

She toyed very briefly with the idea of saying *I know exactly what you are* and thus throwing him off guard. But his question—or at least the way he had asked it—demanded an honest answer.

"Yes," she said, "I'm afraid I do."

"I understand," he said. "At least I think so."

From Christine's point of view, it was not the perfect reply. There was a question in it—a plea that she explain his uncertainty to him and so put him on firmer ground. Which was why, of course, he had lowered his head and closed his eyes. Because it was her turn.

The dull ache of disappointment flowed through her. There had been something genuine about this man, and now he had destroyed it.

"Will you give me some time, Christine?" His head was still lowered, eyes still closed.

"Time?" she said, without expression.

He raised his head, looked at her. "I'm not going to try to talk you into something or out of something. I don't think I'd be able to; you've made that very clear. All I want is for us to take the time to get to know each other. I like you . . . very much. Well, that's obvious, isn't it. I can't say . . ." He paused, considered. "I can't say I like the fact that you're crippled. I don't like it. I wish I had some kind of healing power. I wish I could lay my hands on your head and say 'Rise, walk,' and then throw that damned chair away. But I can't. No one can. Which leaves us . . . here. Nowhere, if that's what you want, and I don't think you do. I know I don't. So . . ." Another pause. "So, I understand. This past month you've been watching me very closely, trying to get a line on what I'm all about, what my intentions are." Again a pause. "I have none —intentions, I mean. Not yet, anyway. Given a little time, though, which is what I'm asking for, I'm sure I'll come up with something." He grinned. "End of speech."

Christine felt like applauding. He had redeemed himself. And the point of it was, he hadn't been trying to redeem himself. His sincerity had been obvious.

And they both realized that it was the beginning of something.

Two years later, they were married.

But there was still the uneasiness, however subtle. And still, on his part, an overprotectiveness that Christine was reluctant to make an issue of—because it was almost an instinct with him, and it would take time to soften it.

This "house thing," as she thought of it, was a good example of that overprotectiveness. *A home of our own*—it was a phrase he used in a tone that approached reverence. And Christine realized it was in reverence of her, or, more correctly, in reverence of her handicap. *A home of our own.* Compensation for all that life had denied her, the gift of privacy and independence in lieu of the gift of mobility.

Fortunately, valid excuses had been easy enough to find: the expense, the neighborhood, etc. They were excuses that, over the past six months, Tim had ultimately been forced to agree with.

Today, however, was the turning point; Christine knew it. Tim's enthusiasm was too great. An argument was inevitable. This place—the "Cornhill Preservation District"—charmed him. The ten square blocks of large Victorian homes and converted gas lamps and cobblestone streets was like a leap backward to a less convoluted, less self-serving, ultimately simpler time. Add to that the fact that houses still in need of restoration were selling for as little as a couple hundred dollars, and Christine couldn't blame Tim at all for his enthusiasm. Here his dream of *a home of our own* was all but assured. Only she—the focus of that dream—stood in the way.

He turned right onto Selbourne Avenue. "The next one," he said, "is a gem. You'll love it." He reached the end of Selbourne Avenue and turned left onto Briar Street. He stopped almost immediately.

The house, like most of the others in the district, was of brick, but it was simple, uncluttered. There was some scrollwork along the roof line and around the windows, but it did little to alter the house's appearance of strength and solidity. There was nothing gingerbready about it.

Christine hated it. It was a hiding place, a fortress, a place to shut herself up in. That was why Tim had called it "a gem," she realized.

"What do you think?" he said. He was smiling, pleased. This was the *pièce de résistance*.

She smiled back, hoping he would catch the falseness of it. "I don't know."

"You don't know? How can you not know? It's perfect, absolutely perfect. It's practically all you need."

"All *I* need, Tim?"

"All *we* need." He was still smiling, was obviously not aware of the implications of what he'd said. "Just the right size, doesn't need that much work, and we can get it for almost nothing. It's perfect."

"Can we talk about it, Tim?"

"Talk about it? Sure we can talk about it. Let's talk."

"I mean later."

He said nothing for a long moment, then: "I'm wasting my time, aren't I." ·

She could hear the disappointment in his voice, the hurt just starting, and it made her suddenly, inexplicably angry with him. She said nothing.

Tim put the car in gear. "Yes," he said, "we'll talk. I want to get this damned thing straight." He pulled away from the house. "It's the same old story, isn't it?"

"The same old story?"

"Yes. You suspect my motives: Tim wants to be the white knight for poor, crippled Christine."

He paused. She said nothing.

"I knew it," he continued. "Jesus, when are you going to learn I've grown beyond that!"

He put the left blinker on, slowed the car. Christine looked ahead, read the street sign: "Longview Terrace."

"Well," he said, "believe what you want. You always have." He turned onto Longview Terrace. "One more," he continued. "Then we'll go. Not that I'm letting you off the hook. We *are* going to talk. Your particular . . . delusion isn't doing either of us a bit of good."

"Fine," she said. It was nearly a whisper.

He glanced at her. "Are you listening to me?"

She said nothing. She was looking out her window; she was very still.

"Christine?"

Again nothing.

He reached across the seat, put his hand on her shoulder. "Honey?"

She turned her head slowly. Their eyes met. He withdrew his hand spontaneously and grinned, suddenly nervous.

"If looks——," he began, and fell quiet: She had turned her head again.

In 1907 Joseph Stearns married Isabelle Morgan. It was a marriage that was several years in the making, a kind of gift to them both: Stearns had just finished law school and felt he could now support a wife.

Owning a house, he believed, was critical to his new role as lawyer and husband; it had much to do with his standing in the community and with his status as a family man. Besides, Isabelle had, long before their marriage, made it clear that she would not accept living in apartments.

In most things, Joseph Stearns was a conservative man. His politics, his religion, his social views all reflected his Victorian upbringing. It dismayed him, therefore, that his tastes in architecture didn't run in the same direction, that the plans his architect showed him depicted, as he called them, "nightmarish monstrosities." He supposed that his hatred of the architecture of the time meant that he was, above all else, a realist, an honest, no-nonsense man. And there was the cost to consider, as well.

In the end, with the grudging help of his architect, he designed his own house. A year later, a couple months after their marriage, Joseph and Isabelle Stearns moved into their new home at 26 Longview Terrace.

From the first day, Isabelle's disappointment was obvious. The house was too small, she said. It was too plain, she said. It was like a box made of bricks. The rooms, all the rooms, gave her claustrophobia. It had no charm, she said.

And Joseph Stearns couldn't help but agree. His first attempt at architecture had been a dismal failure. The house was all but unlivable.

In 1909 Isabelle Stearns died of influenza. A year later Joseph sold the house, at a substantial loss, to a sculptor named Gears. Gears lived in it until June 1922, when he boarded a train for New York City and was never heard from again. The house became the property of Gears's only living relative, his sister, Elizabeth O'Donahue, who used it as an income property. She rented it, variously, to newlyweds and transients and artists who, like her brother, found its plainness oddly appealing.

But, because Elizabeth O'Donahue was a woman to whom the responsibilities of being a landlady were not as important as the meager financial rewards, the house slowly fell into decay. In March 1950, with a week's worth of snowfall on it, the back section of the roof of 26 Longview Terrace collapsed, killing a young mother and severely injuring her five-year-old son.

Elizabeth O'Donahue was successfully prosecuted for negligence, and eventually the house reverted to the city, became a burden, a file number, an eyesore— only one of several hundred such houses in what had then become, and would remain for another decade, the slum district known as Cornhill.

Tim Bennet didn't know how to deal with his wife's silence, because he didn't know the reason for it. If it was a "tactic," it was one he hadn't expected from her and had never before encountered.

He leaned over and looked past her at the small red brick house. "Well," he said, "it's nothing if not ugly."

Christine remained silent, her head still turned, her hands flat in her lap.

"They're going to bulldoze it," Tim said, straining to sound casual, "unless some poor slob buys it pretty soon."

He waited. Still nothing.

"Okay," he said. "Okay." He straightened, put his hand on the gearshift.

Christine looked at him.

"I'm sorry," Tim said, without knowing why, suddenly needing to say something, anything, to soften whatever it was—anger? hatred?—that had tightened her face, transformed it. "I'm sorry," he repeated, putting the car in gear, his hands shaking, his eyes still on her, disbelieving, uncertain.

"No," she said, "I like the house. Can we go inside?"

Tim couldn't believe what he was hearing.

"It looks just right, doesn't it, Tim? Not too big or too small. It's not expensive, I imagine."

"Three hundred."

"Is *that* all?"

And it struck Tim that what he was seeing was an impossibility, that Christine couldn't speak so enthusiastically, so hopefully, without showing it around the lips and eyes, that only venom could come from that face. "It's beyond repair, darling," he said.

She laughed. Lightly. Pleasantly. Laughter that had, so many times before, made him reply spontaneously—without reason—with his own laughter. But now it stopped his breathing momentarily. "Nothing is beyond repair, Tim. It's always just a matter of time. And money."

"Money we don't have, Christine. Money we'd have to borrow. And I don't even know if I have the . . . the expertise to——"

"Buy it for me, Tim. I really do like it. I'd like to live in it."

Tim said nothing. He stared incredulously at her. Her face was a mask of pleading and insistence. And then, at once, he knew what his answer would be, and why: Because he loved her. And because she had asked.

"Yes," he said. He took his foot off the brake, touched the accelerator. "For you, Christine."

"You *will?* Oh, thank you, Tim. Thank you!"

He turned onto Briar Street, then onto Selbourne Avenue. Within minutes, they were on the expressway and heading for their apartment.

Chapter 2

Six months later

Marilyn Courtney pushed at her husband's chest. "Okay," she said, "are you finished?"

Brett Courtney rolled off her and onto his back. "Yes," he sighed, "I'm finished." He inhaled deeply, let it out slowly, and sat up on the twin bed. "It's cold in here, Marilyn." He leaned over, picked his pajama bottoms up from the floor, stood, put them on. "What have you got the thermostat set at, anyway?"

"Sixty-eight."

"I've told you time and again, Marilyn—seventy-two."

She pushed herself up to a sitting position. "You want me to go downstairs and change it? Is that what you want?"

"No. Forget it." He went to his bed. "It can wait." He lay down. "Turn the light off, would you?"

She turned the light off. "I *will* change it if you want, Brett."

"I said forget it; it's all right."

"I mean, if you're cold . . ."

"Oh, fuck." A sigh. "If you want to change it, change it. I don't care."

"Jesus, aren't *you* in a good mood!"

Brett said nothing.

"Did you know we got some new neighbors today?"

Silence.

"Right next door, number twenty-six."

"That shit hole?" Brett grunted.

"Oh, it's not so bad now. The husband's been working on it since June."

"I hadn't noticed."

"Uh-huh," Marilyn said. "Anyway, this young couple moved in today. And the wife—very pretty little thing; you know the type: blonde hair, blue eyes, looks like a Breck girl—well, it turns out she's a cripple."

"A cripple?"

"Uh-huh, wheelchair and everything. Really a pity. I mean, can you imagine——"

"No, I can't," Brett cut in, "and I'd prefer not to."

"I was just going to say, can you imagine what a burden she must be on her husband?"

She waited. Brett said nothing.

"I knew something was up when I saw him building that ramp," she said.

"Ramp?"

"Next to their front porch. Haven't you seen it? My God, Brett, don't you care what goes on in this neighborhood?"

"Not really."

"I thought so. Anyway, I saw him building that ramp and I said to myself, 'Now, what's he building that for? That looks like hell.' And then it occurred to me that the handicapped use ramps like that, and I just knew that somebody in his family was handicapped, and who does it turn out to be but his wife. Can you imagine it, Brett? I'm sure you've seen this man——"

"No, I haven't."

"Well, he was working on that house every chance he got. God knows it needed it. I don't see how you could have missed him. Great big guy, must be six-five if he's an inch, and not bad-looking, either, in a Neanderthal sort of way. And when I saw that poor wife of his, I said to myself, 'What a pity that he got hooked up with her,' because it really did look like she'd been

in the wheelchair a long, long time, if you know what
I mean."

"No." Then, resignedly: "Tell me."

"Well, it looked like it was part of her, like she was
comfortable with it, and he looked like he'd been pushing it a long time, too."

"That's crap, Marilyn."

"Brett, I know these things, these subtle little things.
If you'd take more of an interest in people, you'd
know what I'm talking about."

"I suppose." He was tired.

"And I've seen her before, too."

"Seen who?" He knew who; it was his way of telling
her to be quiet.

"That crippled woman. I don't remember where,
exactly, but I have seen her before."

"Of course you have, Marilyn. You said her husband's been working on that house for six months."

"No, I mean before that. And today's the first time
she's come to that house, anyway. I *know* that."

"I'm sure you do. Other women watch soap operas;
you stand at the windows."

"That's unkind, Brett."

He sighed. "I know it. I'm sorry. Now, please, can
we go to sleep?"

"And another thing: He wouldn't have built that
ramp unless that wheelchair was a long-term thing. So,
you see, she isn't in it temporarily because of some
accident; she's in it for good. Poor thing."

"Marilyn, I'm tired. Can we please go to sleep?"

She rolled over suddenly and faced the window. The
drapes were parted slightly; she could see the Bennets'
house. "They're still up," she said.

Silence.

"They've got a light on, Brett. They're still up. Real
night owls, aren't they?"

Silence. She lifted her head a little, listened. Brett
began to snore—lightly, rhythmically.

She lowered her head. "They're still up," she repeated, in a whisper. "Why are they still up?"

Brett was right, she thought: It *was* cold. She pulled the blanket over her shoulders, brought her knees up. *Real night owls.*

She considered turning over and checking the alarm clock on the table between Brett's bed and hers, but decided not to: She was comfortable in this position.

She saw the light in the Bennet house dim briefly. Someone had passed in front of the window. Probably the husband, unpacking, doing some more work on the house, while she—the wife—slept. Probably a very fragile little thing. Probably had to be on a special diet.

Damn, but it was cold! The house had never been this cold before.

She pulled the blanket to halfway over her head. Soon she became aware that she was shivering. She sat up, leaned forward, unfolded the bedspread, pulled it over her. She felt her teeth chattering and thought how ridiculous that was: Her teeth never chattered. No one's teeth ever *chattered,* for God's sake.

She looked at the Bennet house again, realized there were no curtains on that window. She squinted, but saw little—a white wall with a painting on it; a lampshade.

She sighed—it warmed her—and became aware that the bedroom door had swung open. She jerked her head to the right. "What——"

Her son. He had a blanket wrapped tightly around him. "Mommy, I'm cold. I can't sleep."

Marilyn sat up and switched the light on. She looked at her husband. "Brett?" She looked at her son. "Come here, Greg."

He went to her, crawled into bed beside her.

"Brett?" Louder now, but he continued snoring. *"Brett!"*

He stirred, stopped snoring, opened his eyes, looked

at her, saw his son. "Greg?" he said. "What are you doing in here?"

"He's cold," Marilyn said. "And so am I. Something's wrong, Brett. Go and check."

Reluctantly, Brett swung his feet to the floor. "I told you it was cold," he said. "Where's my fucking bathrobe?"

"Where it always is," Marilyn said. "In the closet. And I wish you'd watch your language, Brett." She nodded at Greg snuggled up next to her.

Brett closed his eyes briefly. "Sorry," he murmured. He got his bathrobe, put it on, and left the room.

Marilyn switched the lamp off. She turned her head, looked out the window. The Bennet house was dark now.

It was incredible, the whole six months. Incredible. And now, just yesterday . . .

Was he seeing her, really seeing her, another facet of her, for the first time? And what was he seeing? He wanted to ask her. He wanted to know; he *needed* to know.

"Christine?" he whispered. He studied the pale oval that was her face. "Christine?" he repeated, no louder.

He decided to let her sleep: It would take an effort to wake her. And it would be cruel; she would lead him to believe that it was cruel, even though she had gone to bed shortly after dinner, a good six or seven hours ago. Usually, that much sleep would have been enough—too much, in fact. She had always awakened before him, always seemed to regard sleep as a waste of time, a necessary evil, always had the kind of driving energy he envied and was also a little afraid of, for her sake.

But it had all changed. Her energy, her passion for living. Changed. Altered.

He thought at first that it was related to her handicap, but (partially out of fear that it was true) quickly discarded the idea.

Now, their first night in their first house, that fear nagged at him. Because, beyond the mandatory "It's nice, Tim, you've done a good job, I like it," she had had absolutely no reaction to the house—as if it were some hotel they would be staying in for a couple weeks, a stopover, and no reaction was required.

It hurt him deeply. A lot of hard work, to say nothing of the money, had gone into this house. And, in most respects, it was hers, had been designed for her comfort. What had been the second floor—consisting of two small bedrooms and a closet-sized bathroom—was now an open loft, his studio. For her convenience, it was connected to the ground floor by a small elevator. But when he'd shown her the elevator and explained how it worked, she had merely smiled in a patronizing way—a smile she had never before used on him.

And it was the same throughout the rest of the house: The floor-standing cupboards in the kitchen—each with its own lazy Susan—sparked nothing but a patronizing smile; the one large bedroom and bathroom on the first floor—a patronizing smile; the wide doorways, the ramp leading to the front door, the swing-in front windows—a patronizing smile.

He studied her face again and thought how beautiful it was despite the . . . exhaustion that had overcome her, that it was even more beautiful than when he had first met her. In the light it had a soft pink glow, a *healthy* glow, the glow of youth.

That glow, when he first noticed it several months ago, had led him to think—foolishly, he supposed—of vampires, or the reverse of vampires—that one had somehow gotten inside her and was sapping her energy and showing its face through her. Had there been an apparent reason for the change that had come over her (she was working too hard, or there had been a death in her family, or she was having a reaction to medication), he would have shared the thought with her in the hope that it would be comic relief for them both. But there was no apparent reason. Only the fact that she had changed.

He sensed movement beside him, very slight. Then he became aware that the tempo of Christine's breathing had altered—from slow and deep to slow and shallow. She was waking.

He turned his head. "Christine," he said aloud. He saw her open her eyes, focus on him. "Darling?" he murmured.

"The house, Tim." She was speaking lovingly, soothingly; it was the first time she had spoken that way to him in months. "Thank you," she went on, her tone the same. "Thank you," she repeated. And she reached over and touched his cheek. A second later she had withdrawn her hand and was asleep again.

January 9, 1961
7:30 P.M.

The baby-sitter smiled reassuringly. "Don't worry," she said.

Evelyn Winter looked briefly, doubtfully, at her husband, then back at the baby-sitter. It was the girl's first night, and Mrs. Winter was having second thoughts about trusting a thirteen-year-old. The previous baby-sitter had been a woman in her thirties; a recent traffic accident had left her bedridden. In the small town, this young girl had been the only replacement immediately available on a long-term basis.

"Yes," Mrs. Winter said, "well, if you have any problems, just call that number we left near the phone."

"I'll do that, Mrs. Winter."

"She'll sleep until we get home, but if she should wake up and start crying, it's probably because she needs to be changed."

"Yes, Mrs. Winter . . . I know."

A pause, then: "You're sure you can handle this?"

"Yes, I'm sure, Mrs. Winter. I've got two younger brothers at home. I've——"

"Okay, then." She pulled the front door open. "We'll be back by twelve, and, as I said——"

"Yes, I know"—the baby-sitter smiled nervously, as if to apologize for cutting in, and waved her arm toward the kitchen—"you left your number by the phone."

Evelyn Winter frowned. "We'll be back by twelve," she repeated. "Help yourself to whatever you like in the icebox." She started out the door, her husband in tow. She stopped. "Oh," she said; she looked back accusingly. "No boys." And she left. Her husband smiled feebly—*Sorry*, the smile said—and followed.

The baby-sitter closed the door quietly behind them. Evelyn Winter, she decided, was a real class-A bitch. And her husband was a weasel.

This job was going to be hell.

The baby-sitter glanced at the kitchen clock: 9:06. Three hours left. "Shit," she whispered. And nothing on TV: "The Lawrence Welk Show," "Gunsmoke"— a lot of crap.

She pulled the refrigerator door open again and peered in, hoping she'd missed something. But no. A couple half-pints of plain yogurt—disgusting—a half-dozen eggs, a bottle of Heinz ketchup, a quart of low-fat milk, the hardened remains of a Mrs. Paul's coffee cake, a dozen or so jars of Gerber baby food. And, except for a pound of chicken breasts and some leaf spinach, the freezer, she knew—she had checked it twice—was empty. She threw the door shut. "Damn

it!" Mrs. Winter might as well have told her to help
herself to whatever might be crawling around in the
damned cellar: "Help yourself to whatever goodies
you find in the cellar, darling. Lots of keen things down
there." The baby-sitter laughed shortly. It was a shrill
laugh, and harsh.

10:15

The child had been crying for twenty minutes. It was
sporadic crying, on and off, and the baby-sitter had
hoped that each time it stopped it would stay stopped.
But it hadn't, and, at last, the baby-sitter realized that
she'd have to do something. "Jesus H. Christ!" she
hissed; it was a curse she had learned just recently, and
she enjoyed the sound of it.

She went into the child's room.

It was obvious to the baby-sitter, even before she
switched the light on, that the child had vomited: The
smell of it hung sour and heavy in the room. It
was a yellow smell, she thought—a very pale yellow
streaked ever so lightly with orange. Some people did
their bathrooms in the same color.

She switched the light on.

The child was standing up in the crib, a Raggedy
Ann doll clutched in her right hand. Her cloth diaper,
heavy with urine, hung around her knees. She had
started crying again as soon as the baby-sitter came
into the room.

"Jesus H. Christ!" the baby-sitter said from the
doorway.

The child stopped crying and stared inquisitively.

The baby-sitter crossed to the crib. She lifted the
child by the armpits, felt the wet diaper against her
belly through her blouse; she grimaced, held the child
away and shook her a little. The diaper dropped to the
floor.

11:45

The baby-sitter sniffed at her fingers and wrinkled her nose. The smell of vomit still clung to them, though she had scrubbed her hands several times. She lifted the bottom of her blouse and sniffed it. She cursed: This job was worth more than a lousy dollar fifty.

She heard the child crying again, got up from the couch, went to the child's room, pushed the door open. In the light from the living room, she could see that the child was standing up in the crib again, that the Raggedy Ann doll was on the floor in front of the crib.

The child looked pleadingly at the baby-sitter, then reached over the edge of the crib for the doll. "Dolly," she said.

The baby-sitter crossed the room, picked up the doll, and pushed it at the child. The child took it and lay down slowly, the doll clutched to her chest.

The baby-sitter crossed to the doorway. She looked back. "Now, go the fuck to sleep!" she said. She flicked the light switch on, then off, on, then off. "To sleep!" And she left the room.

Chapter 3

Marilyn Courtney knew they couldn't see her. During cloudless days, the glaze of sunlight and blue sky made her windows opaque. She had checked. Often she had stood at the downstairs windows and watched as passersby nodded and pointed and smiled at her house, pleased by it, of course, unmindful of the fact that she was there, behind a window, very pleased that they were pleased. And once she had even stood naked in front of one of her windows and seen no change in the nodding and pointing and smiling. That had proved it: In daylight, she could watch and not be seen. At night, she had merely to shut off the lights.

She wanted to hear them talking, to hear what he—the husband—was saying, anyway, because he seemed to be doing all the talking. She—the wife—looked almost glum in that wheelchair. Poor little thing. She didn't even appear to be listening to him.

They must be on their way to somewhere close, she thought, or they would have taken their van. Probably on their way to the market a couple blocks away, or maybe he was just showing her the neighborhood, or maybe she just needed some air.

They had stopped. He was nodding at the house. Smiling and nodding at the house. Marilyn watched, expressionless, enjoying his pleasure.

Tim Bennet often grinned when he was nervous. He didn't know why, exactly; he supposed it was self-defensive, an attempt to deny that he was nervous.

"Why today?" he asked. "I was hoping you could help me with some of the decorating today."

Christine said, "I don't know if I'm up to that, Tim. Tomorrow, maybe."

Tim continued grinning. He nodded at 24 Longview Terrace again, though Christine, in the wheelchair, her back to him, couldn't see the nod. "How do you know if anyone's even home?" He paused only briefly; it had been a stupid question, he knew. "Maybe they're busy with something; maybe they're having lunch."

Christine turned her head a little and looked at the house. "They're not busy," she said.

How can you know that? Tim wanted to say, but it was obvious from her tone that, whether she knew it or not, she believed she knew it. He sighed. "It's our first day here, darling. There's a lot we've still got to do. We have all the time in the world to go around introducing ourselves to the neighbors."

Christine turned her head as much to the left as she could. Tim saw her look at him out of the corner of her eye.

"Just this one," she said. And she smiled. *Humor me,* the smile said.

Tim, sighing again, turned the wheelchair to the right and began pushing it slowly, carefully, up the snow-slick driveway. "Okay," he said. "But I hope they're not making love or something." He chuckled, embarrassed by the inanity.

Christine said nothing.

Marilyn Courtney stepped away from the window. For God's sake, they were coming here, to the house. To introduce themselves, no doubt. To be welcomed to the neighborhood. And they had moved in only yesterday.

Maybe all they wanted was to borrow something: a saw, a hammer, a little coffee, perhaps, some kitchen utensils—one of those things people always find themselves short of when they've just moved into a place.

She looked frantically around the room. She thought, *It's too dark. They'll wonder why there are no lights on, what I'm doing in here with no lights on . . . and with the drapes open on such a cold day.*

She crossed the room, flicked the overhead lights on, hurried back to the window, drew the drapes closed: The sudden shutting of the drapes caused a quick flow of perspiration under her arms and on her forehead.

She studied the room again. And smiled. They would be impressed by it. She parted the drapes a little and watched as they disappeared around the corner of the house. They were going to the side door.

Tim Bennet hoped no one was home. Forty-five minutes or an hour of idle chitchat and instant coffee served in demitasse cups with these very private people was not the stuff that ideal mornings were made of. Very private people, he knew, because in all the months he'd worked on the house, they hadn't once come over to lend a hand or to say hello. He'd seen the husband only a couple times, either coming or going in his big dark-green Mercury Marquis. And occasionally he'd caught glimpses of what appeared to be a woman's form at some of the side windows. Only the little boy—dark-haired and gray-eyed; he seemed incapable of smiling—had ever bothered to say anything to him, and that just a hurried "Hi" or "You gonna live here?" or "My mommy says I gotta get right home," without waiting for a reply.

He looked around the edges of the side door. No doorbell. He knocked gently.

"Louder," Christine said.

"We don't want to disturb them, honey."

"We aren't disturbing them." She leaned forward in the wheelchair and rapped hard on the massive oak door.

And the house itself—Tim's thoughts continued—said, announced, that they were private people. Gray brick and black trim and spiked wrought-iron fence around the sides and front, only the long driveway open. *Good fences make good neighbors,* Tim thought when he first saw it. And everything about the house always so neat and tidy. These were not only private people; they were fastidious. Private and fastidious. Not the kind of people who enjoyed surprise visits by new neighbors.

"Let's go, honey," he said. "They're obviously not home."

"They're home." Quick, certain.

And Tim heard the doorknob being turned. He put on his *How are you?* smile, though he despised it, and looked down at Christine. He saw that she was smiling in the same way. It pleased him.

The door opened.

She was not what Tim had imagined. He had imagined someone thin and pale and with something unmistakably authoritarian, or aristocratic, about her. This woman might have been dowdy were it not for a kind of cold sharpness around her eyes and mouth. Her dark-brown hair had just begun turning gray above her forehead and around her temples, and her skin suggested too much time indoors. "Hello," she said. (Tim detected a whisper of tightness in the voice; he thought he knew what it would sound like in thirty years—a high-pitched crone's screech, grating and insistent.) "You're my new neighbors, aren't you?" she continued. (Her tone of condescension was obvious.) "I'm afraid my husband's not home. He's at work. He's always at work." (And her breasts were huge, hard-looking. They hugged her black cotton housedress in a way that would have been appealing on any other woman; on her, they were merely big and hard-looking.)

"Hello," Tim said. "I'm Tim Bennet."

She offered him her hand. "Marilyn Courtney."

He took her hand, noticed that her flesh was soft and cool; it seemed an anachronism. He nodded to his right. "And this is my wife, Christine."

The woman withdrew her hand and offered it to Christine. Christine took it; her smile brightened.

"I'm very happy to meet you, Mrs. Courtney."

"Please call me Marilyn."

"And call me Christine."

Tim—as if in prayer or thanksgiving—lowered his head momentarily and closed his eyes. Somehow, he could read it in the way Christine spoke, in the way she smiled, in the few words that had passed between her and this woman, she had come back to him, had rid herself of the thing—the vampire—that had been slowly draining her these past six months.

Chapter 4

Sonny Norton was a tall, stocky man in his middle thirties who walked as if he were constantly hurrying somewhere—legs stiff, shoulders thrust up, arms straight and swinging in precise arcs. He had a long, angular face, reminiscent of the Easter Island stones; his eyes and the set of his jaw had that same studied blankness.

The "pictures" he saw had never scared him too much—they had never actually hurt him—but they had made him wonder and worry about himself, because (his sister, Irene, had told him) they meant that he was not only slow but also crazy. Sonny had been able to memorize Irene's exact words, since she used them so often: "You tell people about these things you think you see, Sonny, and they're not going to like you. They're going to say, 'Look at him, he's not only stupid, he's *crazy*.'" Sonny hated that word—*stupid*. It was a mean word, meaner than the word *slow*, which Dr. Fenaway liked to use. Other people liked to use *retard*. "He's the local retard," Sonny had once overheard George Fox say, as if being slow meant he couldn't hear, either. "But he's okay. He'd cut his right arm off for ya if ya needed it. It just makes me a tad uncomfortable having him around, if you know what I mean." And Sonny thought maybe he did know what George Fox meant, but he wasn't sure.

Sonny had heard about the new people in Cornhill. He remembered that someone had told him the names of the new people—their last name, anyway; but he couldn't remember what it was. Names meant very little to him. They were *always* hard to remember, and he found it difficult to understand why other people put so much importance on them. A person's face was important, and his smile, his tone of voice. You learned a lot from those things. But you learned nothing from a person's name. Sonny had once been told that those thoughts were "surprisingly profound," and, of course, he had no idea what that meant. He knew only that they were true thoughts.

He smiled to himself. It was good to be able to think.

He saw that he was approaching the big, dark house where Mrs. Courtney lived, and he remembered the time—a year ago?—he had been passing the house, and Mrs. Courtney's son had been on the sidewalk, and he, Sonny, had said "Hi" to the little boy, just trying to be friendly, and Mrs. Courtney had come running out of the house, and pulled her son to her and almost spat, "Get out of here, get out of here! Stay away from my son!"

The pictures he had seen around the woman had frightened Sonny more than any of the others. Never before had he seen such pictures around anyone. And the feelings that had radiated from her had made him nauseous, as if someone's strong hands were clutching hard at his stomach, trying to squeeze out what was inside.

Ever since that day, even passing the Courtney house made Sonny nauseous, and so he gave it a wide berth, his eyes riveted on the house all the while.

"Hello," he heard, aware that the word was not really a greeting but designed to make him take notice of the person saying it. He turned his head and stopped immediately. The pretty blonde woman was in a wheelchair, her legs covered by a heavy checkered blanket. She was one of the "new people" in Cornhill; Sonny knew it immediately.

"Hi," he said.

"Hi." The woman smiled.

"My name's Sonny." He gestured toward Avenue A, behind him. "I live down there."

"Hello, Sonny. My name's Christine."

Sonny thought that he liked her voice; it was soft, nearly musical. Which is why he was puzzled, confused, that the picture, the memory, should come to him at that moment. It stemmed from the beginning of Cornhill's rebirth, two decades before, when Sonny was still a teenager. Some of Cornhill's old, decrepit houses had been gutted to make them ready for renovation, and people with hammers and saws and truckloads of brick and roofing tile were everywhere.

Sonny had never been allowed to own a pet (they demanded a lot of attention and care, he was told); but that did not stop him from making "free pets" of the numerous stray cats and dogs that then roamed the streets of Cornhill. ("They're my friends," he explained. "I feed them, sometimes, and I pet them. They know me, and I know them.") One day, he came upon a new stray—a huge, short-haired gray tabby sleeping quietly just inside the front entrance of an abandoned house. He watched the cat a while, pleased by the feeling of serenity and comfort it gave him, by its perfect beauty. And then—because he had no fear of stray animals, had always known instinctively which were approachable and which weren't, and because of the good feelings this animal gave him—he leaned over and put his hand on the cat's back and began to stroke it.

Instantly the cat awakened, lashed out at him, and ran into the house. Sonny followed, his intention to apologize to the animal for disturbing it. He found the cat in a second-floor bedroom, cornered it—"I'm sorry, kitty cat, I'm sorry"—tried to understand the new feelings radiating from it, feelings of fear and panic, tried to equate those feelings with what the cat had been only moments before, felt awed by the two so totally different creatures this cat could be.

He leaned over again, certain he could calm the cat and make it into the beautiful, peaceful thing it was.

It took many stitches to sew up his arm and hand. The scars would remain with him for the rest of his life.

Sonny could not understand why that memory should return—and so vividly—when he talked to the pretty lady in the wheelchair. The feelings that came from her were so good, so loving. What could his memory of a cornered and panicked animal have to do with that?

Chapter 5

Christine shook her head slowly, in self-criticism. This wouldn't do. What she had captured here, on the canvas, was not the boy's spirit, not the fire inside him, but only the face he had presented to the world—the innocence and the wonder the world expected of him. The boy she remembered had gone deeper than that—subtly, yes, but deeper. That boy would have been a world burner someday. The boy she had painted would not shape the world; he would be shaped by it.

Her error, of course, was in the eyes. Perhaps she had *wanted* only innocence, only wonder from this boy. Perhaps the thing she had seen in that other boy's eyes had frightened her a little, had made her want to restructure him on the canvas so she could save a semblance of him from the pain that would obviously have been his—a kind of *Picture of Dorian Gray*, only the other way around.

"Does it hurt very much?" the boy had asked, pointing stiffly at the chair and at her legs.

"I don't remember that it ever really hurt," she told him.

There were other children his age playing in the small park, but he had apparently only been watching them from a distance. Not glumly, as though he wanted to but could not be a part of their fun; merely watching.

"Do you come here a lot?" Christine asked.

"No," said the boy. "I come here sometimes."

"To play"—she nodded—"with the other kids?"

The boy glanced around. When he looked back, a soft, almost long-suffering smile was on his lips. "I play with them sometimes, but not a lot."

"Don't you like to play with them?"

The boy's smile sharpened, as if Christine had told him a bad joke. Christine thought the effect, on any other child's face, would have been ludicrous. He said, "I don't think they like to play with me," and he emphasized the word *me*.

"No," Christine said without thinking, "I'm sure you're mistaken."

"No, I'm not," the boy said, and the same *That was a bad joke* smile was on his face. He turned abruptly to his right and, in a minute, was gone.

Christine thought of yelling after him "I'm sorry," but realized the apology wasn't necessary. She hadn't upset the boy, hadn't opened old wounds; he was merely finished talking with her and had better things to do.

She had gone back to the park a number of times in search of the boy, but he had not reappeared. It saddened her a little. She imagined that he was a very lonely child—though, in time, he would learn to cope with it—and that she was one of the few people who would ever know how to deal with him, how to talk with him, how to be his friend.

And then one day, just after her marriage to Tim, she was sitting in the park and a little girl, apparently intrigued by the wheelchair, approached her tentatively, cautiously.

"Hi," the girl said.

"Hello," Christine said. "What's your name?"

"Cecile."

"That's a nice name. My name's Christine."

"You're very pretty," the girl said.

"Thank you. So are you."

The girl blushed. "My daddy says I look like my mommy and he says my mommy looks like a witch."

"Do *you* think your mommy looks like a witch?"

"My daddy says so, but I think he's just kidding."

"Of course he is." She paused. "Cecile?" Another pause. "Cecile, have you seen . . . do you know a little boy . . . he's about your age, maybe a year or two older, and he's about so tall"—she held her hand up, palm down, several inches above the little girl's head—"and his hair is almost as light as mine, and he's very handsome, with blue eyes. The last time I saw him he was wearing a blue jacket." She caught the confusion on the girl's face. "He didn't like to play with the other kids very much, Cecile."

The girl's confusion was replaced by a look that approached sorrow. "Oh," she said, "that's Jimmy Wheeler. He . . . he died."

Christine said nothing. She didn't want to know how he had died; she knew how—in some stupid automobile accident. Not from some disease, not while playing, but from a stupid automobile accident. Somebody had run a stop sign or someone had been drunk, and had killed him. Some stupid slob who would feel sorry about it for a few days or weeks and then go out and do it again. That type had ended Jimmy Wheeler's life. And had left himself, and his own kids—like these kids, these studies in mediocrity—alive.

Christine lowered her head, ashamed by the thought. When she looked up, finally, her eyes moist, the little girl was gone.

It was a bad memory, and it came back to her now, made her eyes moisten again.

She studied the painting, the eyes especially. She wouldn't change it, she knew; she couldn't. For her sake, this was Jimmy Wheeler.

She put the canvas on her lap and wheeled herself out of the room and into the small foyer. She decided that once she had it in a frame, the painting would go on the west wall, to the right of the living-room doorway. Jimmy Wheeler would be undisturbed there; few visitors would bother to stop and look at him. He could watch.

"Damn it!" Marilyn Courtney said. "Damn it!" She could hear the rushing noise the gas jets made, could see the rectangle of blue flame. Upstairs, she had felt the radiators heating up. "Damn it!" So, the furnace was working; it was doing what furnaces were supposed to do. And it wasn't. Which was impossible.

"Appears to be all right to me, Mrs. Courtney," the furnace repairman had told her an hour before. "You got any windows open?"

"Of course not," she answered.

"Well, then, you got your storm windows up? These things are tricky sometimes."

"Yes, we *have* storm windows up."

He grinned an apology. "Sorry, then, I can't help ya. It's not the furnace, I can tell ya that." And he left, taking a twenty-two-dollar check with him.

She thought about calling Brett, then wondered what good that would do: He knew as little about furnaces as she.

She reached up to turn off the bare light bulb hanging from one of the beams, saw that her fingers had been blackened. She grimaced. Cellars were always such foul, dirty, *close* places.

Simple white drapes, Christine thought. Nothing ostentatious, nothing pretentious. Just something simple, to match the room. To match the house. And no rugs. The hardwood floors were all right.

It was a good house. Tim had done a fantastic job with it.

She reached out, put her hand on the window. The glass was warm. Beyond it, a light snowfall had begun. It wouldn't amount to much, she thought. It was like dust falling. Maybe it was only the top layers of the two-day-old snow already on the ground being lifted into the air by a gentle, persistent breeze.

Winters . . . They were hateful. And they were beautiful. They kept her prisoner, kept her out of the parks and off the sidewalks, unless someone—Tim now—was there to help her. But they also slowed things down, or appeared to, brought things to a standstill, and in that they were beautiful. Things that moved—cars, motorcycles, bicycles—were covered over in a heavy snowfall, stopped. Real things became scenes from a picture postcard.

She took her hand from the window. Her gaze settled on the Courtney house. It was a fortress on the outside, she thought, and a museum inside—dust-free, precise, sterile. The old things Marilyn Courtney surrounded herself with had died under her influence. Died, hardened, lost their texture, their warmth, their charm.

She thought she couldn't blame them, really. Marilyn Courtney was that kind of woman. Things died around her. Even the air chilled.

She turned away from the window; she disliked the cruelty of her thoughts. How long had she known the woman, after all? There had been only the half-hour conversation the day before, a conversation that had obviously been uncomfortable for her, for all three of them. So, it was too soon to be making judgments, wasn't it?

Jimmy Wheeler stared at her from across the room. Christine smiled wistfully at him. "Yes," she said. "Okay." And the words made her wistful smile a self-amused one.

January 23, 1961

Joanne Vanderburg was a slimy little bitch, thought the baby-sitter. The thought pleased her; it was right on target, an indictment worth filing away for future use, for the next time the bitch opened her big mouth. Which would be soon, of course: Monday morning, in study hall. The baby-sitter wondered if it would be the "zit" thing again, as it had been earlier today. ("Oh, what is *this?* Is it a *zit?* My God, it *is* a zit! What a pity. It absolutely spoils your face. Are you going through puberty? Is that why you have that *thing* on your face?") It had been a long, painful five minutes before the laughter in the classroom had ended, and then only because Mrs. Beaman had come back.

The baby-sitter wondered just how much her hatred of Joanne Vanderburg had grown in the past few months. Enough that if the opportunity presented itself, she could actually . . . A gentle shove at the curb where the buses pulled up, a well-placed foot at the top of a flight of stairs? Something that required only minimal involvement, something that would be widely thought of as an unfortunate accident. Splat, and that would be it for the damned slimy bitch. No more mouth, no more worries. Splat! The baby-sitter smiled. Maybe, given the right circumstances, she could do it. Just maybe. It was very pleasant to consider.

Fitful crying from the child's room halted the baby-sitter's thoughts. She cursed, stood, went into the room, turned the light on, and moved quickly, with agitation, to the crib.

Her agitation softened when she bent over the crib. The child had stopped crying and was smiling now, obviously pleased by the baby-sitter's presence.

Feigning a grimace, the baby-sitter lifted the child, checked her diaper, and found that it was dry. She laid the child down. "So what's the big problem?" she said. She waited. The child continued to smile at her. The baby-sitter straightened and put her hands on her hips in mock frustration. She felt something soft around her ankles. She looked. The child's pink cotton blanket lay on the floor in front of the crib. She picked it up, covered the child with it, and quietly left the room.

Chapter 6

Tim rolled to his side; he put his arm over Christine's chest. "Hi," he said.

"Hi," Christine said, noncommittally.

A number of phrases came to Tim: *Are you in the mood? How are you feeling? You really smell good. Your breasts feel nice under my arm.* Even *I'm horny, how about you?* He rolled his eyes in disgust. Christ, if he had to talk about it with her first, if he had to convince her, it wasn't worth the effort. They had gone that route for the first six months of their marriage, and their lovemaking had undergone a long, painful transition. Even now, tonight, he could sense something of the aura of those months coming back. He closed his eyes, and their first time together—a long, sweaty, nerve-wracking two hours—replayed itself. He wondered if he would ever forget it; he wondered if he wanted to.

They had been avoiding it for months; it was something, they knew, that could either destroy their relationship or cement it. And then:

"I'm a virgin, Tim. What do you think of that?"

Tim had grown accustomed to her pointed questions, but he smiled nervously at this one. "What would you like me to think of it?"

"That I'm courageous."

"Okay. You're courageous."

"Or that I'm afraid."

Tim hesitated. He would be treading on very unstable ground here. He hoped she would elaborate on her fears, because he had his own, and—damn it!—they were probably not far removed from hers. But she didn't elaborate; she waited. And Tim felt that she had put him on the spot; he told her so:

"You've put me on the spot, you know. You do that from time to time."

But Christine was not to be sidetracked. She grinned. *That's not what we were talking about,* the grin said.

They were at his apartment. With his help, Christine had seated herself in a big, comfortable La-Z-Boy left by the previous tenant. Her knee-length plaid skirt had hiked up considerably on her thighs, and Tim, standing near his small makeshift bar, made a point of noticing.

"You've got marvelous legs," he said, and cursed himself. Of all the things he might have said, all the small erotic, suggestive comments available to him, that one had to be the clumsiest and the cruelest. "I'm sorry," he murmured.

"Why? I *do* have nice legs. Even my therapist thinks so. He says they're a little thin, but he thinks I'm thin, anyway. He says I should eat more." She hesitated. Then: "Please don't be nervous, Tim. I'm nervous enough for both of us."

He went to the kitchenette, got a kitchen chair, brought it back into the living room, and placed it next to the La-Z-Boy. He sat, considered a moment, then put his hand on her thigh. Her upper body shivered noticeably. He withdrew his hand quickly, lowered his head, shook it. "Jesus, Christine . . ." It was as much in admonishment of her as of himself. He felt her hand take his; he raised his head. She placed his hand back on her thigh. "It tickles?" she suggested, and they laughed suddenly—a soft, strained laugh.

He patted her thigh and stood so that his back was to her. "This is all very awkward, isn't it?" he said.

"Yes, it is, Tim."

"Would you rather we just forgot about it?"

"No."

He turned his head, surprised by her response. "No?"

"I love you, Tim. You know that I love you. No, I do not want to stop."

He went back to the bar. "Would you like a drink?"

"Maybe later."

He was about to make himself a gin and tonic. He put the bottle away, sat on a barstool. "So," he said, trying to sound casual, "you're afraid of sex, huh?"

"I don't know if I am; I've never experienced it."

"You're afraid of finding out about it?"

"Aren't you?"

Tim hesitated, momentarily uncertain what her question meant. "I think it could be disastrous for us. And it could be quite beautiful."

"Disastrous, yes. Beautiful? No."

"Christine, darling, we've got to be philosophical about this." Tim was suddenly pleased that he was saying all the right things.

"My paralysis is not a matter for philosophy." Her quick, impatient tone surprised him. "Neither of us, Tim, is so . . . so high-minded that we can overlook it, that we can pretend it doesn't exist. I may be a virgin, Tim, but I sure as hell am not naïve. I've read the books; I've seen the movies. I know what people want from each other—a good *performance*. That's not a value judgment, Tim; it really isn't. I am very, very happy for those people who can *give* a good performance. I'm sure it's very fulfilling. But *I* can't, you see, because, as a matter of hard, cold, and really lousy fact, I am a paraplegic."

"Christine," Tim cut in, "you're not being———"

"Realistic?"

"No. Fair."

"Fair to whom? Myself? You?"

He got off the stool, went over to her, and sat in

the kitchen chair. "Now we're fighting, and that's no way to begin a seduction. At least, that's not the way *I* begin one." He heard her words before she said them:

"Oh? You're very practiced at the art of seduction, are you?"

And he thought, *I deserved that*. "Not really," he said. "No more than normal."

"I wouldn't know about that—normal, I mean."

"That's cute, Christine." His voice was heavy with sarcasm. "Your self-pity is terribly creative——"

"Tell me, Mr. Bennet, just how many women *have* you had here? A dozen? A hundred?"

"Sixteen thousand and two, and they were all marvelous."

She frowned.

"I just love this snappy repartee, Christine."

"Hey, I didn't ask to be seduced."

"And I didn't ask for all this self-pitying, self-indulgent horseshit you've been slinging at me. And, by the way, yes, you *did* ask to be seduced."

She thought about that. "Okay, so I did. Now I've got a headache."

Tim threw his hands in the air: "Jesus Lord in Heaven!" He cupped her face in his hands. She made a feeble attempt to pull away; he tightened his hold slightly. "I love you, I love you, I love you, Christine. And I want to take you to bed." He expected a quick, witty reply, saw that she was trying to form one, but the moment passed. Several moments. And then:

"I'm only a hundred and five pounds," she said, softly. "Think you can lift me, Tim?"

"Well," he began, in a husky whisper, "I haven't lifted weights in a long time, but . . ." He let the remark die. He stood, bent over, put one arm around the back of her neck, the other behind her knees, and lifted.

The effort made him fart.

They laughed all the way into the bedroom.

*   *   *

The laughter stopped abruptly when he lowered her slowly, and with great gentleness, onto the bed.

Christine pushed herself to a sitting position, her back against the headboard. "Your mattress is much too soft," she said, trying for the gaiety of moments before.

Tim said nothing. He sat on the edge of the bed, leaned toward her. His hands went to the top button of her blouse.

Christine put her right hand on his. "Can we . . . talk first, Tim?"

His hands, beneath her hand, worked expertly at the button, unfastened it, started on the second button.

"Tim, please . . ."

He unfastened the second button, paused a moment, then took his hands away from her. He held them up in a mock gesture of surrender. "Okay, okay, we'll go as slow as you want. Do you think I should send out for pizzas?"

"Tim, try to understand." She started to button up her blouse, stopped. "Try to remember what it was like for you—your first time, I mean. Then multiply whatever agony you felt by a hundred, a thousand."

Tim did remember: It happened when he was fifteen. He was visiting a friend whose parents were divorced. An overnight visit. A little past midnight he had gotten out of bed to use the bathroom, and, on his way back to the bedroom, was confronted by his friend's mother. "You have bedroom eyes," she told him, and Tim thought that that was an odd thing to say. "Thank you," he said, and felt her hand on him. The next two hours were, she told him later, his "initiation to manhood." However true or false that was, he thought now, she had given him one of the most marvelous nights of his life.

"Yes," he said to Christine, hoping his lie wasn't obvious, "you're right. It was agony. I'm sorry."

"All I'm asking, Tim"—she put her hand on his

shoulder—"is that we go slow. You don't gulp down a bottle of Dom Perignon, do you?"

"I don't drink Dom Perignon," he said.

"Well, how do you know you're not about to?"

Tim liked that, clumsy as it was. "You're a good talker, Christine." It was a challenge.

He watched several emotions sweep across her face —nervousness, fright, passion. Suddenly, she was breathing noticeably deeper. Her hands went to the third button, then the fourth. She hesitated. "They're not much," she said, and in that instant Tim felt an overwhelming affection for her. She unfastened the last button and pulled the blouse open.

It was not the first time he had seen her breasts. She did not wear a bra, and from his vantage point above and behind her when he pushed the wheelchair, he had sneaked more than a few impulsive glances. He felt sure she had known. Now, seeing her face and neck turn a soft shade of red, he realized she hadn't.

He cupped a breast in each hand; they fit nicely. "They're priceless," he said. Her small brown nipples erected almost instantly. He bent over, kissed her left breast, then her right. A tear hit his cheek; he looked up. She was crying.

"Oh, Christine, I'm sorry. Please . . . forgive me." He sat up quickly, cast about in his mind for something to say.

"Sorry for what?" said Christine. She looked pleadingly at him. "Sorry for wanting me?" She quickly pushed herself to a prone position, unzipped her skirt down the side. "I'm protected," she said.

"Protected?"

"I've been on the pill for months, ever since we . . . Well, I guess I foresaw this evening."

Tim smiled. "Do you mean you can——"

"Tim, I'm not *sterile;* I'm paralyzed."

He bent over her again, pulled her skirt off, started

on her panties, hesitated. "It's not too late," he said.

"Yes it is," she said.

And it had gone badly from there. Not until the second week of their marriage was Tim finally able to complete the act. Misplaced guilt, and the feeling that he was being somehow perverse, that he was actually using her in a selfish, animalistic way, took their toll immediately. It amazed him: He had thought himself more stable than that.

Now, eight months into the marriage, it seemed they often slipped back two steps and went forward only one. This process of acceptance and confidence and sharing, Tim thought, was both hellish and wonderful.

"Tim," he heard, "I'm very horny."

He pulled her to him. Later he would wonder if there was a place in the *Guinness Book of World Records* for the longest-sustained ecstatic lovemaking.

Chapter 7

Brett Courtney whispered, "Shit!" Where was his secretary this morning? Then he remembered: It was Sunday. "Shit!" he repeated.

He felt a twinge at the back of his neck—a migraine just starting. He hurried into his office, sat behind his desk. And waited. The migraine would last at least an hour, and in that time he would be able to do nothing but suffer through it.

He heard a knock at his office door—just one, and soft. A woman, he thought immediately. He decided to wait; maybe whoever it was would go away. The knock came again, and again, slightly louder. Brett grimaced. "Who *is* it?"

A woman's voice answered, "May I see you, Mr. Courtney?"

Brett, agitated, went to the door, pulled it open. "Yes?" And couldn't help staring. The woman was almost impossibly beautiful. The word *stunning* occurred to him, but he rejected it immediately; it implied a momentary shock, a quick surge of deep appreciation that soon dissipated, and this woman's beauty was so much greater than that.

She introduced herself: "My name's Andrea Ferraro. I'd like to talk with you, Mr. Courtney."

He held the door open, watched her step into the office. She studied it briefly.

"Very functional," she said. "I like that, Mr. Courtney." Her voice was high-pitched but exceedingly pleasant; it reminded Brett of his mother's voice.

He gently pushed the door closed. "What can I do for you, Ms. Ferraro?"

She smiled. His migraine, which had been lingering at the edges of his consciousness, vanished. He felt a smile come to his lips.

"Thank you," she said, "but I don't mind the word *Miss*. I've always thought *Ms.* was an affectation." She paused, considered. "In fact," she continued, "I'd really prefer that you called me Andrea."

She crossed the office, sat in a black Naugahyde chair to the left of Brett's desk. Brett watched appreciatively as she adjusted her plaid skirt around her knees—he had always liked plaid skirts—and made herself comfortable. He felt certain her little feminine motions were being done for his benefit; it made him feel good.

"Uh, yes, Miss Ferraro——"

"Andrea," she corrected, her tone a gentle, almost inviting rebuke.

"Andrea. What can I do for you?" He strode quickly, arms straight at his side, to his desk chair, sat, felt a warm, delicious pain he hadn't felt in years. Embarrassment mixed with pleasure flooded through him. Not since his college days had he achieved an erection merely by *watching* a woman. . . .

"Mr. Courtney?" he heard, and became aware that Andrea had been saying something. "You seem . . . preoccupied, Mr. Courtney." There was no puzzlement in her voice. Her tone was one of recognition, knowledge. *I know what preoccupies you, Mr. Courtney, and I'm flattered,* her tone said.

The phone rang—once, twice.

"Mr. Courtney," said Andrea Ferraro, nodding, "your phone——"

"Oh!" He grinned apologetically—"Yes, excuse me" —snatched the phone up, as if in anger, and swiveled his chair around so that his back was to his visitor. He had a good idea who was calling.

"Brett Courtney," he said.

"Brett?" It was Marilyn; he'd guessed right.

"Yes, Marilyn, what is it?" He found that he was speaking in a low, secretive tone.

"It's about Greg. Remember that . . . distasteful matter we discussed last week?"

"Distasteful matter? What are you talking about?" Then he remembered. "Oh, that. Yes, I remember."

"Well, I'm afraid it's come up again."

"Marilyn, I thought we decided to forget it. The boy is nearly ten years old; things aren't the same as when you and I were that age."

"That's very progressive, Brett, but he's my son, too, and if you're unwilling to give me some constructive ideas——"

"My idea is to let it alone, Marilyn. It's normal, it's natural, it's probably even healthy, for Christ's sake."

"You're swearing at me, Brett."

Brett sighed. "I'm sorry; I didn't mean to. I've got one of those damned migraines." It was close to the truth.

Marilyn chuckled shortly, derisively. "Only *women* get migraines, Brett. What you've really got is a severe case of apathy. But that's all right. You want me to handle this situation, I'll handle it."

"Marilyn, can you at least wait until I get home?"

"It's unwise to put off punishment, Brett."

"Marilyn, for God's sake!"

"Good-bye, Brett." She hung up.

Brett slowly replaced the receiver, swiveled his chair around.

Andrea Ferraro was gone.

"Miss Ferraro?" He stood, went to the office door, opened it. "Miss Ferraro?" Nothing. He turned, glanced about his office as if this were a game of hide-

and-seek she was playing with him. He felt suddenly foolish.

He pushed the door closed, felt the ache beginning again at the back of his head. "Jesus Christ!" he whispered.

He went to his desk chair and sat very slowly. The migraine was fully upon him now.

"Honey?" Tim called. He opened the door to his studio, stuck his head out. "Honey, I've got to go down to Hahn's. I didn't realize how low I was on developer." He waited There was no reply from below. "Honey?" Again nothing. He opened the door, stepped onto the landing, and leaned slightly forward over the wooden railing. He glanced around the living room. "Honey?" He saw that she was in the wheelchair, her back to him, in front of the window that faced the Courtney house. "Christine?" Still nothing.

He took the elevator to the first floor, hesitated a moment, and stepped out. "Christine?" he repeated. But she remained motionless, silent.

Was she asleep? he wondered. "I've got to go to Hahn's," he repeated, moving slowly toward her. "I'm nearly out of developer." He put his hands on her shoulders, leaned over. "Christine?"

Silence.

He moved to the side of the chair, put one knee to the floor, his hand on her hand on the armrest.

Placid, he thought. Her face was placid, at rest. She could be asleep, and yet her eyes were open. Not wide, but as if she were thinking something pleasant, as if remembering something that gave her pleasure.

He put gentle pressure on her hand. "Christine?" He stood, grasped her left shoulder, shook it. "I've got to go to Hahn's," he said again, almost desperately. "I'm nearly out of developer."

Silence.

He lowered his head. "Christine," he murmured.

He stood abruptly, crossed to the phone, picked up the address book. What was her doctor's name? After a moment it came to him: Tichell. He found the name and number, set the book down, picked up the receiver, started to dial.

"How's it going?" he heard.

He froze for a second. Then, being sure his body blocked Christine's view, he quietly replaced the receiver. He turned. She had craned her head around and was looking questioningly at him.

"Going?" he said.

"Up there." She raised her head to indicate his studio.

"I've got to go to Hahn's." It was a forced monotone. "I'm nearly out of developer."

She maneuvered her chair around to face him and smiled perplexedly. "What's wrong, Tim?"

"I hate to run out of materials right in the middle of a project, that's all. Especially when I'm on a deadline." He went into the foyer, got his coat, shrugged into it. "I won't be long, just a few minutes."

"Who were you calling, Tim?"

"Calling?" He reappeared in the living-room doorway. "No one. Just time-temperature."

"Oh?" She wheeled herself to the middle of the room, flashed him another perplexed smile, but now it was mixed with accusation. "Something's wrong, Tim, and I wish you'd tell me what it is."

"No. Nothing. Just this crap with the developer."

"You're sure?"

He went to her, leaned over, and kissed her lightly on the forehead. "I'm sure."

Greg Courtney was too numbed with fright to cry. He didn't know what he'd done, precisely, but it didn't matter. This place mattered, because it was dark here and chillingly damp, and if the house itself had always made him uncomfortable—although he had lived in it all his life—the cellar had always scared him silly. The reason was simple: There were things in the cellar that couldn't live above ground, things that came into it from the earth surrounding, things that crowded into the darkness once the light was turned off and the door closed—once the cellar was left to itself. Cellars were for dead things because cellars were below ground.

Greg started to shake uncontrollably. He realized that he was scaring himself, that it was a stupid thing to do, that cellars were just places where furnaces were put, and boxes and old furniture. Sometimes cellars flooded, and then it was a real hassle getting them cleaned up again.

He wanted, needed to cry. The shuffling sounds of the things slipping toward him in the darkness would be covered by his crying. But he was still too numbed, disbelieving, frightened. He thought suddenly how wonderful it would be if he could go to some small point in his mind where the reality of this place would be far beyond him, where he would be out of its reach— invisible, inside himself.

He knew there was a light above him, that it would be easy to reach, but quickly discarded the idea of trying, because the numbing fear in him now was better than what the sudden turning on of the light would show him.

He knew what he should be thinking—about other things, silly things: clowns, unicorns, barber poles. But he found that he could only think the words, and they were really code words for the things that existed in cellars, the things that were slipping toward him in the darkness.

He lashed out suddenly with both hands. The back of his right hand connected with something metallic, and a hot pain settled into his hand and arm. He swore—"Shit!"—and realized it was the first time he had ever used the word. If his mother heard him . . . Pain overcame his thoughts. He knew he had hurt himself. He stumbled toward the cellar stairs, found them, started up. "Mommy?" he called, tearfully. "Mommy!"

The cellar door opened; the sudden light blinded him momentarily. "Mommy, I hurt myself." His eyes adjusted; he saw that the doorway was empty.

He moved quickly up the stairs—the darkness behind, the light ahead, the pain pushing him. And vaulted through the kitchen, into the hallway, then to the entrance to the living room.

Because the curtains were open, he could see that a light snowfall had begun. And he could see that his mother was at the other side of the large room, near the windows, her back to him. "Mommy?" He noticed that the pain had ebbed, that his hand felt merely numb. "Mommy, I hurt myself. So I came upstairs. It's okay, isn't it?"

Marilyn said nothing. Greg saw that she was holding something in her left hand—a sheet of paper.

He moved forward a few steps, stopped. "Mommy?"

Marilyn spoke, her tone even but tense: "I forgave you before, Greg. I sent you to your room, but it was necessary. You had to be punished before you could be forgiven. You understand that, I'm sure. You're a smart boy. You're my son. But this time you have deliberately, *deliberately* defied me. And I cannot countenance that. You understand why, don't you? You understand that if I let you do what you wanted to do, you would eventually destroy me? You understand that, I'm sure." She moved her left hand backward a few inches to indicate the piece of paper she held. Her tone became crisp, demanding: "I see from this . . . this *obscenity* that you have started to destroy me already, to put me out of your heart. And I don't blame *you*, Greg; it's the *animal* in you that I blame. And that animal has to be brought under control. Do you understand that, Gregory?"

"My hand hurts real bad, Mommy."

"I'll explain it to you; you'll understand. You're a smart boy. You're my son." She crumpled the piece of paper slowly as she talked. "You are going through what's called *puberty*. It means you're becoming . . . a man." Her tone softened very slightly. "It's a natural thing, Greg. But it's evil, too, because it destroys the child in you, *my* child. Do you understand?"

Greg did not understand. He mumbled something unintelligible, then fell silent.

"I am letting you come up from the cellar, Greg, but only under one condition." She held her hand out behind her, the crumpled piece of paper in it. "This is the evil in you coming out, Greg—an evil we must keep *inside* you. So, it's clear what you must do, isn't it?" She turned halfway, looked Greg squarely in the eye. "It's clear," she repeated, her tone crisp, demanding, "what you must do, isn't it?"

Greg said nothing. He moved quickly across the room, took the piece of paper from her. He glanced out the window. The snowfall was much heavier now. A storm was coming.

He put the crumpled piece of paper into his mouth, let his saliva work on it.

"That's right, Greg. I told you you were a smart boy. You're my son." She walked halfway across the room, stopped, turned. "There'll be nothing about this to your father."

Greg nodded.

"Good." She paused, then continued: "Supper will be ready soon, and I want you nice and scrubbed before you come to the table. That cellar is filthy."

Greg nodded again.

Marilyn smiled and left the room.

Five minutes later, Greg swallowed the ball of mush that his letter to Coni Weeker had become.

Chapter 8

Christine tried to make herself comfortable, but realized the room wouldn't allow it. She had felt the same way several days before when first entering the Courtney house with Tim, that it disliked visitors, that it was a showpiece not meant to be lived in. Entering this room today, she had been aware of the paths the wheels of her chair made in the expensive oriental rug, and she caught herself glancing at Marilyn Courtney for signs of disapproval. But the woman had been almost cloyingly gracious from the moment Christine appeared at the side door.

Now, regardless of Marilyn's apparent cordiality, Christine sat very stiffly, the corners of her lips turned slightly upward in what she knew was not really a smile.

There was a cup of tea on a spindle-legged cherry-wood table to her right, but, in fear of spilling it, she knew she wouldn't touch it. Marilyn sat cross-legged on a velvet rococo couch between the living room's two front windows.

"It's really very good to see you again, Christine. I very much enjoyed you and your husband's visit the other day. Your husband's a charming man." The condescension in Marilyn's tone was almost palpable.

"Thank you, Marilyn. I think he's all right."

Marilyn grinned; her teeth, Christine noted, were large, straight, and healthy. "That's a nice thing to say, Christine. You and your husband seem to have—

what's his name again? Tim?—you seem to have what I call a playful marriage. And that's all right. In time —you're both quite young—I'm sure your relationship will mature."

Christine's lips moved nervously, trying to form a reply. Marilyn went on, as if in apology:

"That is in no way a judgment of you and your husband as individuals, Christine. I'm sure you are both very fine people, a real asset to the district, unlike some I can name. But that's another matter. No, when I say your relationship will mature, I mean only that it will grow solid, secure, if for no other reason than that it persists. Do you follow me?"

"I don't know. Maybe, in a way."

"I'll explain it all to you while I show you my house."

Christine looked quizzically at her.

"Would you *like* to see my house?" Marilyn said. "We didn't have time for it the other day."

"Of course I'd like to see it, Marilyn, but——"

"Oh." Marilyn's gaze settled a moment on the wheelchair. "Yes. Well, that's certainly not going to stop you from seeing the first floor. And there's plenty to see. I've spent years, literally years, furnishing this house" (Christine fought back a grin; Marilyn had used nearly the same words two days ago), "and it is my pride and joy. I am, by design and by inclination, a homebody, Christine. Women's libbers can go off and burn their bras and work as pipe fitters, but I am very happy, thank you, to see to my house and to my family." (And those were *exactly* the same words Marilyn had used two days ago. Christine had always thought such repetition was a sign of senility. It was also a sign of obsession, she realized now.)

"Let me *tell* you about my house first," Marilyn said.

Christine nodded quickly. "Yes, please do."

"It's authentic mid-Victorian, built around eighteen

seventy-four. The original owners were a banker and
his family. Quite a large family, of course; that's why
the house is so large. His name was Sporrington"—
she spelled it—"and he was a grotesque man. At the
end of his life, he weighed all of three hundred and
fifty-five pounds. He strangled to death at the dinner
table. You'll see the table itself—a genuine Duncan
Phyfe, inlaid mahogany. And while he was dying—
while he was sitting there strangling to death on a
chicken bone, or whatever it was—he stuck the table
three times with his fork. In desperation, I'm sure. The
marks are still there. You'll see them. And"—she
beamed—"I have the fork, too."

Christine grimaced. "Marilyn, I really don't——"

"Duncan Phyfe," Marilyn cut in, "Eastlake, Haviland, Faience Manufacturing, Gillinder and Sons . . .
Do these names mean anything to you, Christine?"

"Well," Christine began, "I *have* heard of Duncan
Phyfe, but I always thought it was Duncan *and* Phyfe."

"No, no. He was only one man, a furniture maker,
of course, and that was his name—Duncan Phyfe. I've
spent literally years furnishing this house, Christine,
making it into the showpiece that it is, making it comfortable for my family. We have few things in this life
to cling to, Christine; the most important, of course, is
the home we live in . . . and the people who live in it
with us." She stood, crossed the room quickly, went
around to the back of Christine's wheelchair, put her
hands on the push bars.

"I really prefer maneuvering the chair myself, Marilyn, when it's possible."

Marilyn backed up a step. "Oh! I *am* sorry. I didn't
know."

"But, if you'd like . . ."

Marilyn stepped back to the chair, bent over slightly;
Christine felt the woman's breasts against the back of
her head.

"Thank you, Christine. It would really be a new experience for me."

"Fourteen rooms," Marilyn announced. They were once again in the living room, Marilyn on the velvet rococo couch, Christine near the cherrywood table; her cup of tea, now cold, was still on it. "You saw only five of them, and I do so wish you could see them all."

"It's a beautiful house, Marilyn. You must be very proud."

"I am proud of *many* things, Christine: my home, my family, my marriage. I am . . . a rock in this little community." She adjusted her dress over her knees. "Have you met my husband?"

"No, I'm afraid not, but I'd like to."

"He's a busy man, a very busy man. He's an insulating contractor, you know. He goes around and insulates houses—not personally, of course; he has a crew of ten men who do the work—and this is the very busiest time of the year for him." She stood, crossed the room to a tall walnut armoire, opened it, withdrew a photograph. She brought the photograph to Christine. "This is my Brett," she said.

Christine smiled as she studied the photograph: It showed Marilyn and a tanned, mustached, patrician-nosed man in his late thirties or early forties—a very good-looking man.

"He doesn't have that awful mustache anymore," Marilyn said. "I told him to shave it off; it made him look so . . . so radical. Don't you think he looks radical?"

"I think he's quite handsome." She felt Marilyn stiffen suddenly, felt tension begin to rise between them. "I mean," she amended, "in a . . . a very distinguished way. A fatherly way."

Marilyn took the photograph from her, returned it to the armoire. She went silently to the rococo couch, sat primly, arranged her housedress. "We use all these rooms, you know. We have occasional visitors and so we need the space. It was quite a chore furnishing each room, but very much worth it." Her tone became low, secretive. "I even have a room of my own that no one knows about, because no one ever uses it. Not even me. Except, of course, when I clean it. I'm saving it."

"Saving it?"

"Don't ask me for what. It's just a big, airy room and it's mine. I guess I'm leaving it . . . uncorrupted." She stopped. Christine saw her focus on something in the archway, and turned her head. Marilyn said, "Come in, Gregory."

Greg Courtney hesitated a moment, then stepped slowly into the room. "I just wanted you to know I was home, Mommy."

Marilyn held her arms out. "Well, aren't you going to give me a kiss?"

Greg hurried across the room and into her arms.

Christine saw the bandage around his right hand. "Did he hurt himself, Marilyn?"

"Don't boys *always* hurt themselves, Christine? He was playing with some of his rowdy friends—some friends I have forbidden him to play with—and he fell and sprained his hand. Thank God it's not a serious injury."

Greg straightened, turned—Christine saw that his face was blank—and left the room.

"And that," Marilyn said, "is my Gregory."

"He looks a lot like your husband."

"Yes, he does; everyone says so. He's my little sweetheart." She sighed. "All right, enough of that nonsense. How would you like some more tea, Christine?"

"No, thank you. I should be getting home."

Marilyn stood. "Yes. We've had a nice afternoon, haven't we? Let's do it again very soon."

"I was over to see Marilyn today," Christine said. "Who?" Tim asked.

"Marilyn Courtney"—she nodded in the direction of the Courtney house—"the woman next door."

"Oh, her."

"You don't like her very much, do you, Tim."

"I really can't say. I don't know her that well, and frankly——"

"Frankly, you don't want to know her?"

Tim thought a moment. "I guess that's true. Yes."

"That's not at all like you, Tim." Her tone was one of question and criticism. "You could at least give her a chance."

"I gave her a chance."

"I mean a *fair* chance."

Tim sighed. "You sound like I decided out of the blue to dislike the woman, as if I didn't have *reasons*."

"You have reasons?"

"Of course I do." He paused to collect his thoughts. "They're pretty subtle. I mean, I can't say that I dislike her because of her political beliefs or because she's a snob or because . . . because she put that ugly fence up——"

"It's not *that* ugly, Tim."

"I think it is, but that's not the point. The point is . . . the point is . . ."

"Yes?" Christine coaxed.

"The point is, she's a phony."

"That's not a revelation, Tim."

"I happen not to like phonies."

"Tim, we're all phonies in one way or another; Marilyn Courtney is just more obvious about it. It's almost as if she wants you to *know* she's a phony, as if she's saying, 'Look, there's a real person underneath all this.'"

Tim was puzzled. "I didn't see *that*, exactly."

"Because you didn't look." She grinned smugly.

"You haven't cornered the market on sensitivity, Christine. Sure there's a real person underneath that mask of hers; a mask has to cover something, after all.

I'm just saying that, in her case, what it covers is probably as lousy as the mask itself."

"That's unfair, Tim."

"Life's unfair."

"Are you ending the argument on that profound note?"

"I didn't know we were having an argument; I thought it was a discussion."

"No, it's an argument, and you've made your point. I guess I don't have the ability to choose my friends wisely. I guess you'll have to choose them for me."

"Don't be stupid."

"I can't help it, Tim. I don't see things the way you do, so I *must* be stupid."

Tim shook his head slowly, in frustration. "What in the hell are you becoming so defensive about?"

"Because . . . because you act as if my handicap isn't . . . isn't just physical." Tears were starting. "You act as if it's . . . as if I'm still a child, as if I'm——" Tears were flowing freely. Tim put his hands on her shoulders. She pushed him away. "But I'm not a child. I'm *not* a child!"

"Christine, please . . ."

She abruptly wheeled the chair around so that her back was to him, put her hands over her face.

Tim went around, gently pried her hands away. "What is it, darling?"

After a long moment, she looked up at him. "I'm sorry, Tim." She grinned pathetically. "That was stupid, wasn't it. Forgive me."

He put his arms around her, felt her tears through his shirt. "It's okay. I understand."

Christine whispered, "I'm glad *one* of us does."

"We won't discuss Marilyn Courtney ever again. Agreed?"

She nodded against his shoulder.

He repeated, "Agreed?"

"Agreed, Tim." Still a whisper. "Agreed."

February 20, 1961

The child opened her door an inch. "Mith King?" she said.

The baby-sitter heard the child and reflected a moment on being called Mith King, liked how adult it made her feel, how truly more than just a teenager. She turned her head. "Yes, what is it?"

"It's cold, Mith King."

"Well, it's colder in here. Go back to bed."

The child became confused. She could feel that it was warmer outside her room. "Blanket, Mith King. Light on."

The baby-sitter did not reply.

"Blanket, Mith King. Light on."

The baby-sitter stayed quiet.

"Mith King, I cold!"

The baby-sitter jumped to her feet, turned, faced the child, pointed stiffly at the child's room. "Go to bed. Go to bed, you freakin' little brat!"

The child's jaw dropped, and trembled; she hesitated, as if in shock, turned, and fled to her room. The baby-sitter followed, flicked the light on, saw the child struggling to climb over the dropped side of the crib: From the crib's mattress it had been easy, but from the floor it was impossible.

"How in the hell——" the baby-sitter started. Then she remembered: When she changed the child's diaper an hour ago, she'd forgotten to lock the side up.

She went to the child, lifted her by the armpits, plopped her into the crib. "Now, goddamnit, you had better go to freakin' sleep!"

The child stared at her, wide-eyed. "Yeth, Mith King. Thorry, Mith King."

The baby-sitter crossed to the door, turned the light out, and left the room.

Chapter 9

Christine wondered if she felt cramped in her little house, if it was really too small, too functional. She wasn't sure. Tim seemed happy in it, and that was important. The district—Cornhill; rich with the aura of another time—was good for his work. "Gets the old creative juices flowing," he had told her, looking a little embarrassed by the inanity. "Any time but the present." She thought it was untrue. His photography had everything to do with the present. In effect, his camera was his soapbox. *Look,* his pictures said, *at what we're doing to ourselves, at what we're doing to our cities. Where is our future?*

And what about her own future? Christine wondered. Her art? What had she been able to do since moving into this house? Only her painting of Jimmy Wheeler, and that was really for no one's eyes but hers —a Jimmy Wheeler she had created out of a quick chance meeting, grief, and wish fulfillment.

The doorbell rang. She felt a little annoyed by the intrusion. She considered not answering, and waiting for whoever it was to go away, but decided that her private thoughts weren't leading her anywhere, that, indeed, they were tending toward the depressive.

She wheeled herself to the door, turned the knob. "Stand back, please," she said, because Tim had installed the door so that it opened outward, toward the back of the small porch. She heard shuffling noises on the porch. She pushed the door open.

The woman was about Christine's age, maybe a year or two older, Christine thought, and quite tall. She had the kind of soft, fair prettiness that would endure well into old age.

"Hi," she said, and smiled warmly. "My name's Becky Foster. We're neighbors."

It was a proclamation obviously designed as an invitation to friendship. Christine's smile in return was spontaneous. She wheeled her chair backward a few feet. "Come in, please." And she was suddenly happy for the intrusion.

"We live in a haunted house," Becky Foster explained. They were in the living room, Becky in Tim's old recliner, Christine facing her from a few feet away. "But then," Becky continued matter-of-factly, "everyone in Cornhill lives in a haunted house."

"I'm fascinated," Christine said, grinning. "Do *I* live in a haunted house, too?"

"It can't be helped." She held her hands out to the side, palms up in a gesture of helplessness. "You buy the house, you buy the ghost. Now, let me see . . ." She pretended to think a moment. "Oh, yes. Your ghost—this is all true—is the ghost of a woman who was killed here about thirty years ago, *over* thirty years ago: nineteen fifty. She was doing something in what was then the kitchen. I got all this from people like George Fox and Irene Norton. They've been here a long, long time, Christine. They're practically fixtures in Cornhill, like the streetlamps." She paused, then: "Where was I? Oh, yes, your ghost. As I was saying, she was doing something in the kitchen, something very domestic, I'm sure, and it was winter, and there was all this snow piled up on the roof——"

"Don't tell me, Becky. You'll scare me to death."

"No I won't; you look pretty tough." Christine liked that. Becky continued: "Lots of snow, must have been ten feet of it." She paused, put her hand up as if to stop herself. "No, that's a gross exaggeration, a *gross* exaggeration. There was no more than five feet of snow on the roof—that's what George told me. Anyway, however much it was, it was enough to cave the roof in, and there she was, this nice domestic woman doing her crude domestic thing in her tiny kitchen, and whoosh!—the roof fell right on top of her."

"That's horrible; the poor woman!"

"Oh, she *was* poor. Everyone in Cornhill was poor in nineteen fifty. But, tell me, have you . . . felt her around this place? You know, thought someone was watching you, felt her presence lurking in doorways, that sort of thing?"

"No, but I'm sure I will now."

"I don't think so. You see, when I moved in about six years ago, I was told all about my ghost—a Confederate soldier, George Fox said. A spy. He made it all the way to my house—no one knows what his mission was; he probably had a lover up here—then he died of pneumonia in what turned out to be my living room. I've never seen him, though God knows I've looked. So I wouldn't worry. There may be a hundred ghosts in Cornhill, a thousand, but no one has actually seen one in the flesh, so to speak." She paused to change the subject. "So, tell me, what do you do?"

"Do?"

"To keep yourself sane."

"Oh. I paint. At least I used to."

"Why *used* to? Don't tell me you've given it up."

"I guess you could say I'm in a slump. From moving, I suppose."

"Am I prying?"

"Yes, but I don't mind."

"You're very honest. That's good—so am I. Maybe

we'll get along." She glanced around. "I don't see any of your work up."

"You should have seen our other place. I doubt there was a square inch of free wall space. But here . . . I don't know. All my work is in storage. Maybe I'll get around to hanging it someday. I haven't really given it much thought."

"Maybe this is a new start—this house, I mean."

Christine thought a moment. "Maybe. In a way it is. Tim says it is."

"Tim's your husband?"

"Uh-huh. Maybe you've seen him."

"Tall, lean, Kris Kristofferson type?"

Christine laughed. "That's the first time I've heard that comparison."

"I've seen him. All the women around here used to take turns gawking at him when he was working on this place." She broke into a playful smile. "Excuse me, Christine. One of my bad habits—at least as far as wives are concerned—is a genuine aesthetic appreciation of good-looking men."

Christine smiled back; this woman was no threat, merely candid. Tim *was* good-looking, after all.

"And," Becky continued, standing suddenly, "on that clumsy note, I must be off."

"So soon?" Christine's disappointment was genuine.

"I told myself before I came over that I had only time enough for"—she put on a quick, passable Groucho Marx imitation—" 'Hello, I must be going,' because I had a few minutes between one little darling and another. I baby-sit, you see, staggered shifts—if you're fond of pandemonium, I recommend it—and my next little darling is due"—she checked her watch—"five minutes ago. She's probably set the house on fire by now." She started for the door, stopped briefly. "May I come back sometime?" She grinned. "When your husband's home?"

"Definitely *not* when my husband's home, but any other time, please feel free."

"Good. I will."

Becky Foster left, and Christine thought she was the kind of person who was easy to talk to, and very easy to like.

Chapter 10

"Mr. Courtney, your wife's on the line."

Brett grimaced. "Okay, Sharon"—his grimace became a look of resignation—"I'll take the call."

Marilyn came on the line immediately. "Brett? It's me."

"What is it, Marilyn?"

"You don't have to sound so testy."

"I'm not testy, Marilyn; I'm busy."

"Too busy to talk to your wife, I suppose."

He sighed. "No, Marilyn."

"I just wanted to talk with you, Brett. I just wanted to have a nice conversation. I won't take up too much of your time."

"Uh-huh."

"I thought you should know: There's some kind of . . . I don't know, some kind of draft in the house, and I can't seem to find out where it's coming from. I've checked everywhere——"

"Did you check the attic? The top half of the window that faces the street falls open sometimes. I guess I should fix it one of these days."

"No, Brett, I didn't check the attic, but I don't think——"

"Check it first, then let me know."

"I'm sure you're wrong, but I'll check it if you want." A pause, then: "Oh, and that little crippled girl came over again today."

"Little crippled girl?"

"Christine Bennet. She lives in that ugly little house next door. I've told you about her."

"Oh, yes."

"Quite a nice girl, too. A little shy, perhaps a bit too introspective for my tastes, but——"

"Marilyn, I have to go now. There's a client coming in shortly and——"

"Okay, Brett, I get the message."

"Check that window, like I said."

"Okay, Brett."

"Good-bye, Marilyn."

It would have to be done, Marilyn realized. And she'd have to do it, much as she disliked the idea. It *was* possible that the attic window had fallen open, as Brett said, and that the winter air was moving into the house.

It was no big thing, she told herself. She could run to the top of the stairs, run to the window, close it—if it *was* open—and then run back downstairs. No big thing.

Why, then, was the idea so terrifying? Why, she asked herself, was she convinced that something was in the attic waiting for her?

"Because I'm a stupid shit!" she said aloud. Because *things* waited in attics, just like *things* waited in cellars and in locked rooms and in old, abandoned houses.

She glanced at the phone. Maybe she could call Brett back and say, "The attic door's locked, Brett, and I can't find the key." Then she'd go lock the door and hide the key. But it was no good. Every lock inside the house worked with one skeleton key, and there were at least a half-dozen doors in the house with skeleton keys in their locks. Brett knew that.

"Oh, for Christ's sake!" Marilyn was rapidly coming to the conclusion that there was no way out of it, that she'd have to put aside her fears. That she'd have to go into that damned attic.

She took a deep breath. "Stupid shit," she repeated.

No, the house isn't at all drafty; it's just my imagination, just my imagination. But that didn't work, either. The flow of cool air was obvious, even here on the first floor.

She left the living room, took the stairs quickly, nearly at a run, walked briskly to the attic door.

And found it open. Wide open.

"Oh, for Christ's sake!"

All this anxiety, this apprehension, just because the goddamned attic door was open. "You really are a stupid shit, Marilyn."

She peered up the stairs, thinking that with what courage she had she might be able to check that window after all. It was obviously open; the draft here, in front of the attic door, was like a stiff wind.

Marilyn shivered.

She mounted the attic stairs slowly at first, then, halfway up, more quickly. She paused on the top step and studied the window across what looked like an acre of attic floor. *Christ, all that junk we put up here and it still looks like an auditorium!*

The window, she saw, was open. Brett would be so smug about that, about being right.

She started across the attic floor to the window. She wished, suddenly, that she'd brought a coat up with her; it was so cold here, so chilling.

She winced as a bead of perspiration trickled from her forehead into her eye. She rubbed the eye angrily. "Goddamnit!" she hissed. "Goddamnit!"

She closed the window with effort and cursed Brett's laziness. The window had probably needed fixing ever since they moved into the house. Well, she'd certainly see to it that it was fixed now, even if it meant calling a damned repairman.

She started back.

How long was it since she'd been up here? she wondered. Five years? Ten? Of course, there had never been a reason to come up here. Brett had seen to it that whatever needed storing got stored either here or in the cellar. Or got thrown out. Most of this stuff—the lamps that needed rewiring, the baby furniture, the worn-out chairs, the boxes of letters and postcards could be thrown out. It was all junk. Some women would call it *memorabilia;* that was just another word for *junk.* The past is the past. Why leave its props lying around cluttering things up?

Several seconds before she could see it, she knew that the attic door was closed. She had heard it close.

She stared at it a long while. Perhaps it would open suddenly through the force of her will. That would spare her a lot of agony, because, of course—she knew it, there was no doubt of it—the door was not just closed; it was locked.

"My God," she murmured.

She took the first step, paused. "Please . . ." And the second. "Please . . ." *Of course it's locked. Something's locked it. Something wants me locked in here.*

She listened to her thoughts, and that portion of her consciousness told her she was being an ass.

She found that she was halfway to the door, and so drenched with sweat that drops of it were falling to the stairs, making small, dark circles on the old, dry wood. *A firetrap . . . This place is a firetrap.*

She reached for the knob, saw that her hand was trembling, felt certain now, as she had guessed all the way down, that *something* was behind her, at the top of the stairs, that it was biding its time, waiting for her to discover that, yes, the door was locked before it started down the stairs—very slowly, very casually, while she cringed in a heap. Waiting.

She turned the knob, pushed.

The door swung open. She stared at it disbelievingly. It was an illusion; it *had* to be.

The door started to close again; its hinges made little rasping noises.

She ran through. Down the stairs to the first floor.

Brett, she knew, would tell her the answer. "Simple," he'd say. "The draft from the open window was keeping the door open. When you closed the window, there was no more draft, so the door closed." And she would agree, reluctantly; otherwise he'd gloat.

And keep the truth to herself.

"Brett, would you do me a favor?"

"If I can."

"Would you take that stuff in the attic—it's all junk —and put it on the curb? Or give it to the Salvation Army? It's just cluttering the house up, and we're never going to do anything with any of it."

"That's a big job, Marilyn. Maybe we could have a garage sale."

"Peasants have garage sales, Brett. Besides, it's all junk—every box, every scrap of clothing, every piece of furniture. Unless we plan on using it, it's junk."

Brett sighed. "Okay, I'll go through it one of these weekends. I'll see what can be thrown out and what can't."

"Besides . . . rats could hide in that stuff."

Brett laughed. "I doubt that the Cornhill Neighborhood Association would let any rats in, Marilyn."

"Does that mean you're going to put it off, like you put off fixing that window?"

"I'll fix the window, Marilyn. This Saturday. And while I'm up there, I'll have a look around."

"Can I consider that a promise?"

"Yes, it's a promise."

Chapter 11

Greg Courtney thought of pretending he hadn't heard his mother call to him. If all she wanted was to ask if he had put his boots, gloves, hat, and coat away, then maybe he could just go up to his room and be by himself for a while. He could listen to some music or read a little. Maybe he could lock the door and read again the note he'd gotten yesterday from Coni Weeker.

"Greg, I am talking to you."

Greg hung up his coat, made sure everything else was in its proper place, and went into the living room.

Marilyn was in the big wing chair near the front windows. The curtains were drawn; one dim lamp had been turned on. She smiled. "Sit down, Greg. There." She nodded at a settee near the entranceway.

Greg sat and folded his hands over his knees.

After a full minute, Marilyn said, "Do you love me, Greg?"

Greg answered the question immediately: "Yes, Mommy."

Marilyn smiled more broadly, as if amused. "That was too quick, my Gregory. I want you to think about it. I want you to ask yourself what love really is, what it means to you, and then decide if that is what you feel for me. Do you understand?"

"Yes, Mommy."

Marilyn sighed. "Greg, you mustn't be afraid of me. I'm not going to hurt you. Now, *are* you afraid of me? Answer truthfully." Another smile, one intended to put him at ease.

"Did I do something wrong?" Greg asked.

"We *all* do wrong things from time to time, Greg. But that doesn't answer my question, does it?"

"No."

"So answer it."

"I'm not afraid."

"You're not afraid of *me,* Greg?"

"No, Mommy."

"Good." She leaned forward, and, in a tone that Greg had never heard from her before—an objective observer would have called it insistent, pleading; it merely confused Greg—said, "Now, *do you love me,* Greg?" She held up her hand, palm out. "Think first, and think hard." She waited.

After what seemed the proper interval, Greg said, "Yes, Mommy."

Marilyn's face tightened. For a moment, Greg thought she had wanted him to say no, he didn't love her.

"And what does that mean, Greg? What does love *mean?*"

Greg was confused. He said nothing.

"Greg, I asked you a question. What does love *mean* to you?"

"I don't . . . know," Greg said haltingly. "I guess . . . I don't know."

"I guess it means *shit,* doesn't it, Greg!" Marilyn was screeching now. "Shit, that's all! Just shit!"

Greg could say nothing.

Marilyn stood so abruptly that she pushed her chair back several inches along the bare floor. Greg jumped at the harsh scraping sound it made.

"You'd better jump," Marilyn hissed. "You'd *better* jump!"

"I'm . . . I'm sorry."

"I'm sorry, I'm sorry!" She was breathing hard.

"Up . . . to your room!" She pointed stiffly toward the hallway. "Up to your room! And you know when to come down, don't you!"

"Yes, Mommy."

"When I *say* to come down, isn't that right?"

"Yes . . . yes, Mommy."

"Now, go!"

Greg left hurriedly, awkwardly; he stumbled several times on the way.

March 13, 1961

Mrs. Winter had noticed it before but ascribed it to her imagination: Just before the baby-sitter was due to arrive, her child grew very quiet and moody. Attempts to find out why had been unsuccessful. Mrs. Winter decided to question the baby-sitter:

"I'm not suggesting anything, you understand. It just seems strange. . . . Well, she's normally such a happy child. Everyone, even strangers, comments on what a happy child she is."

The baby-sitter looked startled. "Do you mean she's been . . . complaining about me, saying things?"

"No, of course not, that's not it at all. It's just that——"

"I do love her, Mrs. Winter. She's a beautiful little kid. I actually look forward to coming here so I can be near her. That probably sounds kind of silly from a teenager, but it really is true."

Mrs. Winter sighed. "Yes, well, maybe she doesn't like to see us leave; maybe that's it."

"Sure it is. I mean, I'm just the baby-sitter, but you're her mommy and daddy."

"Uh-huh." Mrs. Winter frowned a little. Something about this girl troubled her; she couldn't pinpoint what it was, exactly. If she were an older girl, a young woman, Mrs. Winter thought, it would be her subtle pretentiousness; but, in a girl so young, it was hard to accept. This girl couldn't possibly possess that sort of sophistication. She was just a teenager, for God's sake —someone concerned with giggling at boys, and with the disasters of acne, and with her just-starting menstrual periods. She couldn't possibly have already acquired the guile and the anger and the hostility to be guilty of what, deep in her heart, Mrs. Winter suspected. "Uh-huh. You're probably right." She opened the door. "We'll be back at the usual time."

"Enjoy yourselves," said the baby-sitter.

The child backed up a step, obviously frightened.

"I think you and I had better have a little talk," the baby-sitter snarled.

The child backed up another step, and another.

"Come here!" the baby-sitter demanded.

The child stayed where she was.

"I *said* come here! Now!"

The child stepped forward.

The baby-sitter snatched the Raggedy Ann doll from her.

"My doll!" the child protested.

The baby-sitter grinned. "No, it's mine, for now. And what you're going to do is go to your room and stay there alone until I'm certain . . ." Her grin softened. "You love your dolly, don't you? But you love your baby-sitter more, isn't that right? You wouldn't want to see her go away." *Damn!* she thought. If only she didn't so desperately need the lousy dollar fifty this freakin' job got her, she'd tell Mrs. Winter to shove it!

The child suddenly started crying—a pleading, desperate cry, and the baby-sitter realized the precarious position she'd put herself in. She held the doll out to the child. "Take it. You think I'd really keep it from you?"

The child hesitated, confused.

"Take it!" the baby-sitter repeated.

The child took the doll and smiled as if the baby-sitter had done her a kindness.

"See, now," said the baby-sitter, "I do love you, don't I?"

Chapter 12

It was the first time Marilyn had visited, and Christine felt vaguely self-conscious; her little house couldn't possibly measure up to Marilyn's ideas about what was and what was not acceptable in Cornhill, ideas she'd made quite clear the last time Christine visited her:

"You can see, of course, what we're trying to do here, can't you? It's not that we're trying to recapture the past—that would be stupid, and impossible. We're trying to create . . . I guess you could call it a sanctuary, a place outside what some people refer to as the real world." She laughed derisively—a high-pitched, shrill laugh. It made Christine uncomfortable. "But, of course, the real world *is* what you create for yourself, isn't it? We have created . . . castles out of the decay of the past. And that is our world."

And Christine felt sure the woman had cast a deprecatory glance in the direction of her house.

Marilyn nodded at the small open closet to the back of the foyer. "Can I put my things there?" she said. She slipped out of her sable coat, bent over, started removing her transparent slip-on boots (*Old lady's boots,* Christine thought).

"Yes," she replied. "It's nice of you to visit, Mrs. Courtney . . . Marilyn."

"Well, I don't get out very often, but it's not very often I get a nice new neighbor, is it. I don't mind admitting"—she hung her coat up, set her boots neatly beneath it—"that my house gets a little wearisome from time to time, almost claustrophobic, if you can believe that. So, occasionally, I like to get away from it."

Christine wheeled her chair into the living room. Marilyn followed, stopped, looked about thoughtfully.

"You know, dear," she began, "for as long as I can recall, this house has been Cornhill's last eyesore, the . . . pimple on the queen's nose, so to speak. And when your husband—what's his name again?"

"Tim."

"When Tim started working on it, I said to myself, and to Brett, 'He'll never do it. He might as well tear it down and start from scratch.' " She paused, looked momentarily ill at ease.

"Marilyn, is something wrong?"

"No." She smiled weakly. "It's just very . . . close in here, isn't it?"

"Yes," Christine answered apologetically. "I'm sorry——"

Marilyn cut in: "Never mind." Strained cheerfulness. "What was I saying? Oh, yes. But he surprised me—your husband, I mean—he really did, and I'm glad."

"Thank you, Marilyn, that's very kind."

Marilyn leaned over and patted Christine's shoulder. "It's not kindness, dear, it's the truth." She straightened, looked around again. Her gaze lingered on Tim's photographs on the living room's west wall. "He's very good, isn't he."

"I think so."

"Very good indeed. A little depressing . . ."

"It's all in your perception, I think."

"That's true." And with those words, Christine knew, Marilyn had dropped the subject.

"Would you like some coffee, Marilyn, or some tea?"

"Coffee's fine, if you're up to it."

"I'm up to it." She wheeled herself into the kitchen,

became aware that Marilyn was making a show of looking the living room over.

"Christine," she called, "have you met the woman on the other side of you? Becky Foster. Tall woman ... pretty, in a burlesque kind of way."

Christine set the kettle on to boil. She wheeled herself to the kitchen doorway, stopped there. "Yes. She came over a couple days ago. She's nice, very intelligent."

"Intelligent?" Marilyn seemed not to understand. "I don't know about that. I imagine she's intelligent." She paused, put her forefinger to her pursed lips, as if in reflection. "But I'll tell you this"—her lips still pursed, her forefinger still up—"I'll tell you this"—she put her hand down—"I'd be very, very careful around her if I were you. I mean, you're an awfully pretty girl, aren't you, and, well, let's face it, essentially helpless in that wheelchair. If you were not impaired ..."

"I prefer the word *handicapped,* Marilyn." Christine hoped her tone had been instructive, not severe.

"I'm sorry; handicapped, then. . . . If you weren't handicapped, I wouldn't mention it. Well, yes, I'd mention it, but only as a matter of *fact,* as something you should know. I wouldn't put it in the form of a warning."

"A warning? I don't understand."

Marilyn looked surprised. "A girl of your obvious sensitivity and you don't understand?" She paused as if gathering energy, as if Christine had suddenly taken her aback. "Well, then, let me explain myself." She gestured toward a brown wicker chair near a window that overlooked her house. "May I?"

Christine nodded. "Of course."

Marilyn sat in the chair, prepared to cross her legs, decided against it. She fingered the arm of the chair. "Very rustic," she said, more to herself than to Christine. She looked up, nodded at the window. "I prefer being near a window, you know. I always have."

Christine nodded again.

Marilyn went on: "Yes, about our mutual neighbor —Becky Foster." She paused dramatically. "She's a lesbian, Christine. Everyone knows it."

The kettle started whistling.

"Excuse me," Christine said, and went back into the kitchen. Marilyn followed.

"My," she said, "this is all very ingenious, isn't it."

"I have special needs," Christine said.

"Of course you do. And your husband has done a marvelous job. Perhaps he missed his calling. Carpentry seems very much his realm, don't you think?"

"His father was a carpenter, and his grandfather."

"Well, that explains it, doesn't it." She saw that Christine had prepared the coffee. "I'll take my cup, dear." Christine gave it to her. "Thank you."

Chapter 13

Greg Courtney struggled out of sleep. Someone was talking to him, or someone *wanted* to talk to him. Or someone was watching him.

He opened his eyes, stared for a moment at the ceiling, then turned his gaze toward the window. He saw something small and dark—darker than the night sky —hit it, heard a tiny pinging noise. Someone had thrown a pebble at the window.

Still groggy with sleep, he got out of bed, faced the window, started toward it. A larger pebble hit it. He stopped, felt the need to say something—"Who's there?" or "Stop throwing things at my window." But he said nothing.

He moved closer to the window. He could see a streetlamp now. The sight of it comforted him a little, and he wondered offhandedly why he needed comforting.

The night looked cold, cold enough to hurt, the kind of cold that would make him stick to anything metal (the way, he thought, his tongue once stuck to a Fudgesicle). He could not imagine anyone wanting to be outside on this night. No coat or hat or boots would keep the cold out.

Out of the corner of his eye he caught the suggestion of quick, stiff movement. He turned his head, looked. The night remained still. No traffic moved. There was not even a breeze. Across the way, smoke from the chimney of the small brick house next door moved straight up, like a thick gray string standing on end. Greg stared at the string a long while, trying to find the point where the breezes high up caught it and scattered it and made it into smoke again.

At last he gave up the game. He wondered why he'd gotten up in the first place. He went back to bed. He was asleep quickly.

Chapter 14

Becky Foster laughed. It was a nice laugh, Christine thought—a warm and subtly sensuous laugh. Somehow it indicated a woman very much in touch with herself, an intelligent and sensitive woman. But these were virtues Christine had already noted, during their first short talk a week before.

"No," Becky answered, "I can't say I feel a part of the 'new elite.' " (It was a phrase Christine had used in an offhanded reference to the residents of Cornhill. "I feel like I'm part of the new elite here, don't you?" she'd said, in a joking tone.) Becky continued: "And that makes me kind of an outcast. You're just about the only friend I've got in Cornhill, Christine." She paused briefly. "Which do you prefer, 'Chris' or 'Christine'?"

"Believe it or not, 'Christine.' I know it sounds awfully stolid and formal, but 'Chris,' I don't know, it's not me."

" 'Becky' is me, Christine. 'Rebecca' is a name some nurse scrawled on a wrist tag twenty-five years ago; or maybe it just read 'Baby Girl Holmes.' 'Holmes' is my maiden name." Christine nodded. "And ever since they took that name tag off . . . well, ever since I had a say in the matter, I've been called Becky. Do you think I look like a 'Becky'?"

"You don't look like a 'Rebecca.' " Christine studied her with mock seriousness. "Nor do you look like a

'Becky,' if you want to know the truth. *Do* you want to know the truth?"

Becky grinned; she was growing to like this Christine Bennet quite a lot. "I don't know; can I handle it?"

"Oh, sure. It's not the truth, anyway."

"Then, let's have it."

"You are definitely," Christine told her, "a 'Marietta.' " She nodded solemnly. " 'Marietta Munson'— that's your cosmic name."

"My cosmic name?"

"Uh-huh."

"Should I change my driver's license and credit cards?"

"Only if you're going to be pulled over by cosmic cops or shop in cosmic stores; otherwise you'll confuse everyone and we'll have chaos. You don't want chaos, do you?"

They both laughed suddenly, more because of the friendship they realized was forming between them— laughter was as good a cement for it as anything—than of Christine's joking.

Marilyn Courtney turned the knob on her bedroom door and pulled. The door wouldn't open. She pulled harder. Her hands, damp from sudden sweat, slipped from the knob and she stumbled backward. Her foot connected with something soft but rigid. She looked; it was the edge of the oriental rug. "Shit!" she muttered, aware that she was falling.

A moment later she was on her back on the floor. She lay still. Had she broken anything? It hadn't been much of a fall, she told herself.

Why is the door stuck? Did someone lock it? Who would lock it?

She stood shakily, stared at the door.

The room began to change.

She reached for the doorknob, grasped it. *Who would lock the door? And why?*

She felt the room changing around her, felt the air grow heavy and hot and humid. Midsummer air.

She turned the doorknob; it turned partway and stopped.

The air was unbreathable now. Marilyn could hear herself wheezing. "Brett?" she managed. "Greg?"

She leaned heavily against the door, barely able to support her own weight. And tried the knob. It wouldn't turn.

"Marilyn?" she heard.

She felt her knees buckle, felt them hit the floor hard.

"Marilyn, get away from the door!"

Marilyn's accusation had been on Christine's mind ever since Becky's arrival. Christine had pushed it to a far corner of her consciousness, because even if it was true, it was hardly on a level with "She's a murderer" or "She beats her kids." But, much as she disliked the fact, it was an accusation that intrigued her. If it *was* true—and she believed this—it would have no bearing on their new friendship.

"Becky . . ." she began, and fell silent: She couldn't ask her outright. It wasn't the same as asking, "Do you dye your hair?" There was an implicit judgment in this question, like asking a stranger on the telephone, "Are you black or white?"

Some things just didn't matter.

Obviously, Christine realized, this did matter. *Damned hypocrite!*

"Something's on your mind," Becky observed. "Want to share it with me?"

Very sensitive, Christine thought. *Very perceptive.* "It's something I was told."

"May I ask by whom?" Becky's tone grew noticeably stiffer. "Can you tell me that?"

"I wish I could, Becky, but——"

"Was it by Marilyn Courtney?"

Christine hesitated briefly then: "Yes, to be honest."

"She told you I was a lesbian?"

"Yes." Christine was sorry she'd broached the subject.

"And if I were?"

"Are you?" Sorrier still for those two harshly judgmental words.

"No. Does it matter?"

Christine was taken aback by the question. *Does it matter?* It sounded so much like a left-handed accusation: *Did you want me to be what Marilyn Courtney says I am, Christine?*

"Does it matter, Christine?" Becky repeated.

And Christine understood. Some things just didn't matter. If the friendship was genuine, if the possibilities were genuine, some things just didn't matter. Christine smiled, relieved.

"Accept my apology, Becky. Sometimes my mouth makes up for my other shortcomings."

"I can't accept your apology, Christine, because it isn't necessary. And I can't see that you have any shortcomings to make up for."

Simply stated, Christine thought—*affectionate and honest.* She was glad she had a friend in Cornhill.

Marilyn Courtney felt her hands hit the floor. She was on all fours now, trying hard to breathe, wheezing with the effort.

"Marilyn, get *away* from the door."

"Bre . . . Brett?"

She found herself being pushed across the floor as Brett freed the door from the jamb. Then she was on her side; the bottom of the door caught the tips of the fingers of her outstretched left hand. "Brett," she screeched, "stop it!"

"Marilyn, move away from the door."

"You're pinching my fingers, Brett!"

Brett released pressure on the door. Marilyn pulled her hand from beneath it.

And found that she could breathe.

"That was pretty stupid, Marilyn. You know that door sticks."

"Don't call me stupid, Brett. I thought you'd fixed the damned door."

"I thought I had, too. But that's not the point, Marilyn. The point is, you panicked."

"I didn't panic. I . . . I lost control for a moment."

"You panicked, Marilyn. How many times have I asked you to see someone about your claustrophobia? What does it take to convince you?"

"Brett, I do not have claustrophobia. We've talked about this before. I thought we'd settled it."

Brett sighed. "Have it your own way, Marilyn. Have it your own way. But next time I might not be there."

"There won't be a next time, Brett. And of course you will."

Chapter 15

Sonny Norton stopped and looked hard at the big house. He didn't like to think that it scared him, because then he would remember why it scared him, and remembering that would scare him all over again.

"Hi, Sonny."

The boy was pulling what looked like a brand-new sled loaded with bags of groceries. Sonny said "Hi," smiled a big, friendly smile—the only kind of smile he knew—and watched the boy pass. When he was several yards down the street the boy waved once, without looking back. Sonny waved. Then his gaze returned, automatically, to Marilyn Courtney's house.

Fear settled over him. He closed his eyes tightly, as if that would stop the pictures that always came.

He groaned, loud enough to make the boy turn and look back questioningly.

Then, despite his closed eyes, Sonny saw the pictures start.

Marilyn Courtney scowled. *What* was that retard doing now? She rapped sharply on her living-room window—as she had when the neighborhood kids cut across her lawn, before the fence went up—trying to get Sonny's attention. His eyes remained tightly closed, as if he were in unbearable pain.

Marilyn stared disbelievingly at him. God, he had a nerve! It was like he was putting a curse on her and on her house.

She rapped on the window again, harder; she winced, thinking the window might break. There was no reaction from Sonny Norton. She muttered "Goddamnit to hell!" and started for the door.

Sonny did not understand what he was seeing, though he tried. He did not understand who the scarred, ugly woman was, or why she sat smiling—like a snake smiles—in the big golden throne, or why he smelled things burning. Living things.

He had never seen the woman before. He wanted to yell to her, "Stop it! Stop it!"

She was merely smiling, and commanding the living things around her to burn. But he could not see the flames, only inhale the smoke.

"Stop it! Stop it!"

And the woman's gaze fell on him. Her smile widened. He felt the burning start, deep inside his head. He screamed.

The scarred woman vanished.

"Get out of here!" he heard. He opened his eyes. "Get out of here!"

He saw Marilyn Courtney standing before him, a fur coat thrown over her shoulders, spittle on her lower lip. "Get out of here!"

Sonny's mouth fell open. He turned. Ran.

"Creep!" he heard. "Lousy, perverted creep!"

He ran hard. And heard that word repeated over and over again—*Creep! Creep! Creep!*—although Marilyn Courtney had long since turned and gone back into her house.

April 3, 1961

The baby-sitter wished she could cry, then realized that it wouldn't help, that it couldn't erase what had happened, that even ten years from now her memory of

what Joanne Vanderburg had done today would be as
vivid as it was at this moment.

She stared blankly at the TV. She had turned the
volume down and the TV was silent, which was what
she wanted. Silence. To plan her counterattack. The
idea that it would be a counterattack pleased her: It
made this thing between her and Joanne Vanderburg a
small war—so, whatever the bitch got, she deserved.

Joanne Vanderburg! After today, the slimy little
bitch deserved whatever she got. The "zit" thing three
weeks ago had merely been a stupid joke, easily forgotten. But today . . .

Maybe she could turn her in to the police. It was
possible. After all, the bitch had—what was the word?
—*assaulted* her. No, that wouldn't work: The bitch's
father wouldn't let her be put in any "special school."
And it probably wouldn't get that far, anyway.

Maybe she could do to Joanne Vanderburg what
Joanne Vanderburg had done to her. She rejected the
idea immediately: It would be asking for a lot more
trouble than it was worth. The bitch was a year older
and twenty pounds heavier and had a whole flock of
sleazy friends.

The baby-sitter lifted her sweater to just below her
neck, lifted her bra, and gently probed the dark, silver-
dollar-size bruise at the side of her right breast. ("My,
but aren't they popping up nicely! Look at that, girls.
Aren't they popping up nicely?") *Jesus!* It hadn't been
so much the pain, she thought—although there had
been plenty of that and still was—as the embarrassment, the agony of knowing that her classmates had
been watching, some giggling, others—especially the
boys—transfixed, while she clutched the breast with
one hand and tried in vain to push Joanne Vanderburg
away with the other.

The bitch's timing had been perfect. First, at the end
of the study hall, when people were crowding toward

the door, there had been the "knock-the-books-to-the-
floor routine—casually, of course, and with a great
deal of innocence. Then, at precisely the right moment,
when everyone's back was turned, a quick sideways
motion, elbow extended. The baby-sitter remembered
screaming abruptly. But the real agony began the moment those who hadn't yet left the room turned to
watch. To be amused.

She put the bra back in place, and the sweater.
Joanne Vanderburg would pay, and pay dearly. Joanne
Vanderburg was——

The baby-sitter became aware, suddenly, that the
child was crying, had been crying, in fact, for many
minutes.

She stood, muttered a recently learned obscenity,
went to the child's room, and pushed the door open
hard. She switched the light on.

The child was standing up in the crib. Her pink
cotton blanket was once again on the floor.

"For Christ's sake!" said the baby-sitter. Each Friday night for the past three weeks she had had to re-
trieve the blanket a half-dozen times. It was like a
stupid game, the baby-sitter thought. "Once more," she
said, "and that's it! Understand?" The child smiled
tentatively. *"Understand?"* the baby-sitter repeated,
harsher, louder. The child's smile vanished.

The baby-sitter checked the child's diaper. It was
only damp; a change could wait. She laid the child
down, stooped over to pick up the blanket. The Raggedy Ann doll was beneath it. She cursed again,
through her teeth, and kicked the doll. It landed against
the wall beneath the back end of the crib.

"Dolly!" the child pleaded. "Dolly!"

"You don't care about it," the baby-sitter said
through clenched teeth, "so we're just going to leave it
where it is."

"Dolly!" the child said again.

The baby-sitter threw the blanket over the child, turned, went to the door. and put her finger on the light switch. "One more time!" She flicked the light off, then on. "One more time!" She flicked it off again, then on, then off. And left the room.

Chapter 16

Greg Courtney heard the sharp pinging noise and immediately remembered the night a week before. He lay still, waiting. Soon he heard the pinging noise again. Somehow it seemed more urgent, louder.

He swung his feet to the floor, sat quietly another minute, considering. This night seemed even colder than the other one. Frost had started on the outer edges of his window; he imagined he could hear tree limbs cracking beyond it, telephone wires snapping, stray dogs and cats dying a quiet, cold death.

"Greg?"

It had been like a whisper, Greg thought—a shouted whisper, as if whoever had said his name was on the bed with him.

"Greg?"

He stood, went to the window, looked out.

His first thought was that the boy should have a heavier coat on, and some gloves, boots, a hat. He had to be frozen stiff in that blue jacket and with only sneakers on his feet. But he was smiling.

Greg shivered. He thought about getting his robe. Then he saw the boy wave to him. *Come down here,* he was saying.

"Greg!" Greg heard again.

Suddenly a vertical shaft of white light fell on the window from behind him. He turned his head sharply.

"What are you doing out of bed at this hour?" Marilyn marched across the room, grabbed his arm. Her gaze fell briefly on the side yard. "Who's that?" she said, and decided in the next moment that she had seen nothing, only what her sleepiness and her frustration with Greg and the frosted-over window had shown her. Nothing.

She led Greg to his bed, ordered him into it. "You get up again, young man, and we'll do more than talk."

"Yes, Mommy." Greg heard the sniveling tone in his voice. "I'm sorry."

"You should be."

She left the room.

Greg got back to sleep an hour later.

Chapter 17

Brett slowed the car and turned sharply right. A white saltbox house appeared. Abandoned now. He glanced ruefully at it; it was unpleasant to imagine that the owners of the house had died years ago. They had been a beautiful, generous couple, well into their seventies, obviously still very much in love:

"Come in, come in." His name was Ralph Hauser, his wife's name Eileen. They were short, rotund people —cherubic, Brett remembered thinking. Cherubs with wrinkles and stories to tell. Ralph Hauser pointed at Brett's car, at the steam wafting into the still, warm morning air. "I see you got a little problem there."

Brett nodded sullenly. "Afraid so." He introduced himself and Marilyn. They were on their honeymoon, he explained, and wasn't this a hell of a thing to happen on someone's honeymoon? Ralph Hauser laughed: "Sure it is, sure it is, but you'll be on your way soon enough. After you have some breakfast, we'll call Ernie's Garage and we'll say you're a friend of mine and Ernie will give ya extra-good service."

The saltbox slipped past. Brett glanced back, saw the jagged scorch marks above the second-floor windows. He grimaced. *Things change,* he thought. *Things change.*

Ernie's Garage appeared. Brett thought of stopping for some gas and wondered idly if Ernie would remember him. He looked at the gas gauge, saw that he had

half a tankful. He looked up; Ernie's Garage was behind him, the cottage ahead. Only a couple miles.

Andrea Ferraro's call had been a complete surprise.
Though he hadn't put her out of his mind since their
first meeting a week before—it would have been impossible—he had relegated her to a position of pleasant unimportance. Her sudden appearance in his life
had been an anomaly; he hadn't expected it to be repeated. And then her phone call:

"Mr. Courtney?"

The voice was familiar, but he couldn't place it.
"Yes, who's calling?"

"Andrea Ferraro." A pause. "Do you remember
me?"

He noted something taunting, something inviting, in
her tone. "Yes," he answered, his voice low. "I remember you." And he could think of nothing else to
say.

"I'd like to talk with you, Mr. Courtney."

"Yes."

"Today, if possible."

"I'm here till——" He reconsidered. "I can cancel
some other appointments, Miss Ferraro, if it's urgent."

"*Andrea,* Mr. Courtney."

"And call me Brett."

"All right . . . Brett." Another pause. "I could meet
you. I'd like that."

"Meet me? Where? I don't understand."

"You have a cottage on Canandaigua Lake." It was a
statement.

"Yes, but how did you——"

"I'd like to meet you there, Brett. In an hour, if
possible. Is that possible?"

"But the cottage has been closed up for nearly five
years."

"Are you saying you can't meet me there, Brett?"
Again that taunting, inviting tone.

"I don't know, I . . ." But he did know. He had

known ever since their first meeting. This woman did not merely appeal to him; she possessed him. From her first word to him, her first look, she had possessed him. He was bewildered by it. His intellect told him that such things did not—could not—happen that way. Sixteen years of fidelity to Marilyn had to mean something, otherwise those years were a waste, a blank; it was nearly like throwing life away, and that was an immoral, perverse thing (if there were gods watching over him, they would punish him). And yet he knew what he would say to Andrea Ferraro, what would happen in the next few hours.

He prayed the roads would be clear, that the forty-mile trip to the cottage would take no more than an hour. "I can meet you there, Andrea."

"In an hour, then," she said, and hung up.

An amorphous blob of darkness had come up to the north—a storm in the making. Brett wondered if it would bypass the lake. Storms usually did, though when they hit, they hit very hard. He remembered the last time he had been at the cottage, in July '74. A bad time—for him, for Marilyn, even for Greg, barely more than a toddler. The vicious summer storm had trapped them in the cottage for two days. Brett thought now that the enforced togetherness in such a confined space was what had started their . . . emotional separation. He laughed aloud at the phrase. Who was he kidding? He and Marilyn had become strangers to each other. Then he thought that people do not become strangers. They may become friends, but they do not become strangers. You don't stop knowing a person; you either get to know him better, or you admit that you've never really known him at all.

He stopped suddenly. He had passed the cottage. He craned his head around, put the car in reverse, and backed it up in quick, short bursts. He turned into the gravel driveway, stopped again, put the car in neutral.

Why am I here? What am I doing here?

He concentrated his gaze on the cabin's weathered front door. He thought—unreasonably, he knew—that Andrea was inside. Waiting for him. And then he thought what a fool he had been. It was all some kind of joke, a ruse to get him out of the office, Lord knew why.

"Hello, Brett."

He turned his head slowly, disbelievingly, to the left. He saw her face.

"Why don't you turn the car off, Brett?"

It was as if he were seeing it for the first time, as if he had been wandering through some elite gallery of beautiful faces, had turned a corner and come across her face, and the gallery had fallen to ashes around him. Where did the beauty of that face begin? The mouth? The eyes?

"Turn the car off, Brett." He thought her voice was suddenly louder. Such a delicious, musical voice it was, the kind that could put a wailing child to sleep with one word, but touched subtly, powerfully, with sensuality—a voice that said so much about her and yet— of course, of course—only as much as she wanted known.

"Brett, please turn the car off!" She was shouting now; he was sure of it.

He noticed then, from the roar of the engine, that he had the accelerator halfway to the floor. He took his foot from it, turned the ignition off.

Andrea Ferraro stepped back, away from the door.

"No, Mrs. Courtney, your husband is out of the office at the moment."

"What do you mean, 'out of the office'?"

"He left about an hour ago. I'm afraid he didn't say where he was going."

For Christ's sake, Marilyn thought, why did she always have to deal with incompetents? "You are sup-

posed to be his secretary, Miss Diehl. You are supposed to find out where he's going when he leaves
during the day."

"All I can tell you, Mrs. Courtney, is what he told
me, and he told me nothing."

Marilyn hung up.

It was a small cottage, very much like the thousand
others that dotted the lake's shoreline. Outside, it was
a uniformly weathered gray; it might always have been
gray, Brett thought—the people who built it thirty or
forty years ago had probably used gray, weather-beaten
wood. But they had built it to last, had known what
the lake winds, moisture, blown sand, and insects could
do. The cottage, in a foot of midwinter snow, stood
straight and solid. It surprised Brett a little: He had
supposed that without the periodic care of people, the
cottage would have moldered away by now.

He fished a key from his pocket, held it up for
Andrea to see. "I never thought I'd be using this
again," he said, aware of the trembling in his voice.

"Can we have a look around first?" she asked.

"Aren't you cold? I know I am." He wondered if he
sounded too eager, if he was rushing the moment.

She put her hand on his, took the key from him. Her
slight smile said, *All of these moments are precious.*
"I've always enjoyed cold weather, Brett; it makes me
feel alive." Then, suddenly, she hesitated, as if confused.

Brett frowned. Her look made him nervous. "Is
something wrong, Andrea?" He waited. She said nothing. "Andrea?"

She looked quickly to her right, then to her left. "I
don't know," she said, just above a whisper.

"Andrea, are you all right? Andrea?"

A cold wind from the lake rounded the corner of the
cottage and hit him, hard. He started to shiver, tried to
force himself to stop, couldn't. "Damn it!" he breathed.

He reached for Andrea's hand; she seemed not to notice.

"I don't know," she said, not to him but to herself. She looked up at him, through him.

"Andrea?" he said. He forced himself to smile encouragingly. "I need you, Andrea." He wondered what had prompted the words. Her look? "I need you, Andrea."

She seemed not to hear him.

He saw the key lying on a bare spot of ground near her foot. He stooped, picked it up, stood.

"Help me," he heard. And knew Andrea hadn't said it, though the voice had been hers. He stared at her mouth expectantly, as if the movement of her lips would come now, several seconds later. He saw her lips part slightly, saw her smile.

"You look upset," she said, her concern obvious. And slipped her hand in his. "The cottage will wait, Brett. Let's go look at the lake, okay?"

"Uh . . ." Brett managed.

"I think the lake's as beautiful now as in the summer, don't you?"

Yes, he thought. "Yes," he said.

"And it's quiet."

"Very."

She tugged gently at his hand. They made their way to the back of the cottage.

The wind from the lake was colder here. It hit in rapid bursts, quieted a moment, then hit again. It was a sadistic wind, Brett thought. It allowed not quite enough time for his body to renew the warmth it had just lost, then took that little bit away. It was a killer wind. A smart wind.

He put his arm around Andrea's waist, tentatively at first, until he felt her body relax against his. Then his body relaxed.

"It seems colder here," he told her, "than anyplace

I've ever been. Maybe it's the abandonment, maybe that adds to it." He nodded toward the next cabin, several hundred feet to the south. It was a small, squat, neglected structure. Its tar-paper roof sagged now under the weight of old snow.

"A family of five used to come here during the summers," Brett said. "Then, one day they went out on the lake in their little boat and a storm came up." He paused, looked at the lake again, saw a car on the ice near the opposite shore, about a mile off. "They were all drowned." Another pause. "Good people, too."

"That's not a nice story," Andrea said, and he realized immediately that she wasn't chiding him; she was merely making a statement of fact. "It makes me a little sad."

He saw that her gaze was on the car that had gone out on the lake.

The wind hit hard, sustained itself. Brett felt her shiver beneath her suede coat. He pulled her closer to him. "Let's go inside."

"Yes," she said.

Inside, Brett found that the smaller of two lake-facing windows had been broken, probably by vandals. A nest of spiders had been established in the sink; a number of dull-yellow egg sacs lay waiting for spring. "I'll get rid of them," he said.

"No," Andrea said. "They're doing no one any harm. Besides, spiders are good for a house."

Brett smiled. "My mother used to say the same thing."

"You loved her very much?"

Brett hesitated, memories flooding back; his eyes moistened. "Yes," he said finally, and sought to quickly change the subject. He gestured at the small wood stove standing on a square of red bricks. "There should be some firewood around the side of the cottage. Most of it's probably wet, but there might be some we can use." He noticed for the first time the faint smell of mold and disuse. It would grow stronger as the fire heated up the small room, he knew. He glanced at the bed. The blue-and-white crazy quilt—a wedding gift from Marilyn's aunt—was still on it, and two uncovered pillows. It would be a cold bed. And there would be something cloyingly familiar about it: Marilyn's smell would probably still be on it.

He grinned sheepishly. "It's not much, is it."

"Does it matter?"

No, he thought, it didn't matter. Andrea's presence seemed to dispel the mustiness and the stench of bad memories. "No," he said.

"It's a place for us to be, Brett."

"You don't mind that I was here with my wife?"

"If it's going to bother you, yes I do mind. *Is* it going to bother you?"

"I don't think so." Simple. True.

She took off her coat.

"Has he come back yet, Miss Diehl?"

"No, Mrs. Courtney, but I'll have him call you when——"

"Just tell him I've been trying to reach him. If he wants to call me, he'll call me."

"Whatever you say, Mrs. Courtney."

"That's right, Miss Diehl."

Chapter 18

A winter fog—chilling and beautiful—and Sonny Norton thought it was sad that only he would see it.

It was one of those mornings, a Sunday morning, that he woke early, just before sunrise, when he could leave the house without his sister knowing and go out and enjoy how the morning air felt inside his chest, how the houses looked in that light—all that sand-blasted brick and shiny roofing tile and polished stained glass flattened out—one-dimensional, as in a painting, a painting that shifted its colors slightly while he watched.

It was simpler, easier then to feel that Cornhill was his, and when the people started waking (he thought he could hear them waking, each of them turning to a husband or a wife or a Teddy bear or a doll and saying, "Good morning, I love you"), it was because he was there to see it. Without him, Cornhill would go on sleeping. It was a game; he knew it was a game.

Now, with the ankle-high winter fog standing motionless on it, Cornhill had changed again. The brick roads and sidewalks were gone. Getting from one place to another was just a matter of wishing.

A converted Victorian gas lamp nearby winked out. Though he couldn't yet see it, Sonny knew that the sun was about to rise. Soon his people would begin waking up.

April 24, 1961

It was a silly concept—*boyfriends*. A waste of time. Sluts had boyfriends. Joanne Vanderburg was a slut and she had a dozen boyfriends. It was obvious why: Christ, she looked like a freakin' whore! Only assholes would want to have anything to do with her. Bill Williams was an asshole and he had a lot to do with her. And who *was* he, anyway? He was nobody. If you thought about it, his real name was William Williams, and that was just plain stupid. Who in the fuck would give their kid a name like William Williams? Maybe if they knew beforehand that he was going to be an asshole they would. If the doctor said, "Mrs. Williams, your son is going to be an asshole, no doubt about it," they would name him William Williams.

Well, William Williams would get his, and not just from Joanne Slimebag Vanderburg, either. He'd get his so he'd never forget it. She wished—what was a good disease?—*scurvy* on him. And . . . and *syphilis*. Yeah, syphilis was good. Lots of pain. Lots of . . . agony.

"Mith King?"

"Why aren't you in bed?" Maybe his cock would fall off.

"Thirsty, Mith King."

"I don't care if you're freakin' dried up! Get back to bed!"

"Thirsty!" The child was whining now.

The baby-sitter jumped to her feet, pointed stiffly, tremblingly, toward the child's bedroom. "Get back in there! Go on! And if you ever whine like that again . . ." But the child had turned and fled to her room moments before.

Yeah, his cock would fall off, like he had leprosy or something.

Chapter 19

The words were almost precisely in the center of the sheet of memo paper, the handwriting small, the letters tight and neat: "The cottage. At four."

Brett picked the note up from his desk. He reread the words several times, as if missing something each time. Finally, he folded the note and put it in the pocket of his suit jacket. He pressed his intercom button. "Sharon, were there any visitors while I was out?" He had left the office to have lunch.

"No, Mr. Courtney."

"Thank you, Sharon."

He took the note from his pocket, began unfolding it. And realized, at last, who had written it.

He went to the outer office, stopped at his secretary's desk. "Sharon, I'll be out for the rest of the afternoon."

"Yes, Mr. Courtney. And if someone should call?"

"I'm on a bid, that one in Honeoye, and I can't be reached."

"Yes, sir."

The driving was slower this time; the trip seemed interminable. A severe winter storm had been forecast, and the roads were jammed with people trying to make it home before the storm hit. Brett hoped it would hit soon after he got to the cottage. Soon after he and Andrea had settled in. He knew there was a store on the way where he might get the firewood they'd need, and some groceries for dinner (that would be cozy;

maybe the store would have candles, too). He'd have to invent some plausible excuse, something Marilyn would believe. But that was for later, much later.

Now he was a man possessed, a man with a purpose, and with happiness in view—short-lived though it might be. The feeling was magnificent.

It struck him that he couldn't remember what Andrea looked like. The word *beautiful* came to him, and he knew that it fell pitifully short of describing her, but the contours and lines of her face (were her eyes round or oval, were her cheekbones high, was her nose slightly upturned?) would not come together in his mind.

He let his mind relax. Perhaps that would unlock his memory. It didn't, and he felt suddenly troubled, somehow inadequate, as if, in not being able to remember Andrea's face, he had insulted her.

"Damn!" It seemed imperative that he remember; otherwise this impulsive drive would be for nothing. He'd get to the cottage and find it empty.

Except for the other memories. The ones he would never lose. The ones that involved Marilyn. (For him, it had been the start of a small adventure—the gravel road leading to the cabin impassable because of the torrential rains, the summer storm whipping into an insane frenzy all around. Brett knew there was little real danger: The area's drainage systems were good, and the cottage was high enough above lake level that the possibility of flooding was remote. And so he had worked himself into a genuine good humor. The storm was bad, yes, he told Marilyn, but the cabin was solidly built. Why not just enjoy being away from the rat race for a few days? It was what they had planned, anyway.

He hadn't planned on Marilyn's claustrophobia.

At one point—during the peak of the storm—she had even left the cottage. "I'm going home," she announced. "If I have to *walk* the whole forty miles, I'll

walk it." And she was out the door. It had taken Brett
a full half-hour to get her back inside.

The storm ended the next day. And so, he realized
now—eight years later—had their relationship.)

He turned, finally, onto the gravel road. Here the
traffic was sparse, the road all but empty. There were
a few year-round residents, their cottages uniformly
small and gray and tired-looking, much like his own.
He decided that he enjoyed the lakeside in winter. It
was dreary, yes, and cold, but it was also dead quiet.
The cacophonous squeals and screeches of summer
were months away.

He remembered. Andrea's face was as clear in his
mind's eye as his own.

"Andrea," he whispered, because, even in memory,
her beauty was breathtaking.

He hit the brake pedal hard; the car came to a
jolting stop.

A moment later, Andrea opened the passenger door
and got in. "Hello, darling," she said.

Brett stared incredulously at her; words would not
come to him.

"I enjoy a winter walk, don't you?"

"Yes," he managed. "I almost . . . hit you."

She smiled reassuringly. "But you didn't. You
couldn't." She nodded at the road ahead. "Shall we?"

He put the car in gear.

Minutes later, they were at the cottage.

It had been the best—by far the best. Nothing even
came close. This had been . . . beyond words. Brett
smiled at that. He had, on occasion, imagined lovemaking that was beyond words, lovemaking that required not even the grand excuse of an "I love you,"
however passionately said. This had been (and still
was) lovemaking that needed no excuse. And Brett realized that all his lovemaking, all his life, had needed

some kind of excuse: It was release; or a child was wanted; or it was to break the monotony (because there was nothing on TV); or because it was Saturday, the night for lovemaking. Always some damned excuse.

Until now.

This past half-hour.

And into this very moment.

Afterglow . . . He had never before had the time for it, he realized, and he had wondered what it was, precisely. Now he knew.

Then he thought that he was not enjoying it as much as he could. because he was analyzing it.

He squeezed Andrea's shoulder affectionately.

And enjoyed.

"We're staying the night, aren't we, Brett?"

It had been a half-hour since their last lovemaking. Were it not for the yellow light of the kerosene lamp on a table across the room, they would be in darkness. Brett picked his watch up from the floor: 7:10. He chuckled. Christ, he had never had any idea how easily time could slip away, how ecstasy could negate it. He thought, *She's the fountain of youth.* And felt her chuckling with him.

"We both are," she said.

He sat up in the small bed, swung his feet to the floor, felt her fingers moving down his spine. He shivered involuntarily, enjoying her touch.

"Yes," he said, "we're staying the night."

He stood, crossed to the lake-facing window, peered out. There were a half-dozen feeble lights burning on the opposite shore, and a pair of lights—headlights, he realized—moving on the frozen surface of the lake. The storm had bypassed them. "Damn," he whispered.

"Is something wrong?" he heard.

"No," he said, his mind suddenly caught up with possible excuses for Marilyn. "It's just that I forgot to pick up firewood. And we're going to get hungry later on."

He felt her hands on his buttocks. He had always enjoyed that kind of touching; now it reminded him that he was naked and cold.

"Let's go get the firewood, Andrea." Something tense in his voice; he hoped she hadn't noticed it.

"I'll stay here Brett. I'll wait for you." Her hands left his buttocks. "I like it here."

He turned, faced her, saw that she had slipped her black lace panties on and now was stepping into her jeans.

"Okay," he said, surprising himself that he was not giving her an argument. He supposed it was the image that he enjoyed—the image of this remarkable, beautiful, sensuous woman waiting in this tiny cottage for him to return with the firewood and the food. It was such a fantastic, noble image, as if they had both been magically transported to another, less complex time— a time without Marilyn, without excuses. "I won't be long. The store's only a couple miles away. I hope it's still open."

He got into his clothes quickly.

At the door, Andrea kissed him lingeringly.

"You livin' here year round?" asked the store owner. "'Cause if ya are, I can arrange to give ya some credit —that is, if ya got an income. Ya got an income?"

"I'm only staying the night. Thanks." He paused, looked around. "Where's Mr. Francis? Did he sell out?"

"Naw. He died, 'bout five years ago. A stroke."

"That's too bad. I liked him."

"Didn't know him, myself. Now, what was it ya wanted again?"

"Firewood. Mr. Francis used to carry it."

"Sorry, we gave that up. Somethin' else ya wanted?"

Brett sighed. Without firewood, a stay overnight in

the cottage would be close to suicide. "No," he said. "Thanks anyway."

"We got charcoal briquets. Maybe you can use those. They's cheaper than firewood."

"No," Brett repeated. "Thanks again." He left.

He sat in the car—the motor off, the headlights on —for several minutes. Something was wrong; he knew it. It was obvious in the way the cottage door hung slightly open, in the memories that flooded back to him—here, now—memories of Marilyn and of Greg, and not of Andrea.

Something was wrong.

He turned the headlights off, got out of the car, moved slowly, resignedly to the door.

He opened the door, stepped in.

The cottage was empty. Andrea had left him. Her offer to stay while he went for the firewood and the food had merely been some kind of excuse.

He saw the note. She had put it on the table, beside the lamp. He picked it up.

"It's not time yet," he read. "She still has you."

He reread it again, and again, increasingly and naggingly certain that there was something very, very familiar about it, though he couldn't imagine what. Finally he put the note in his shirt pocket.

Chapter 20

The dream was rapidly becoming a nightmare. Greg had many nightmares—nightmares about suffocating and drowning and falling. They were a part of "getting older," he was told, something like "growing pains," though he had no idea what growing pains were, only that they couldn't be as bad as the dreams.

He awoke from the dream with a deep sense of relief, as if he had just stopped gagging on a piece of stringy meat, and opened his eyes wide.

The boy was at the other side of the darkened room, near the closet door. He brought his hand up level to his waist and waved once. "Hi," he said. "I was wonderin' when you were gonna wake up."

Greg asked, "How'd you get in here?" Because it was a two-story drop to the ground, and his window was locked, and there were no vines to climb up on the side of the house.

"I'm a vampire." the boy said matter-of-factly. He took a step forward. "I changed into a bat and I flew in through the window." He smiled broadly. "If you don't believe me, I can do it again."

Greg believed him: He had seen vampires before, in his dreams, and some of them were like this boy. His mouth fell open.

The boy chuckled, amused by the effect of his joke. Greg's mouth clamped shut. The boy's chuckle quickly became an earthy, mature laugh. It made Greg feel very foolish.

Brett hoped Marilyn wouldn't wake, see that he was not in bed with her and come looking for him. He had so few private times—certainly not at the office, and even more certainly not in the hours after he came home, before sleep. Marilyn would not understand his need for "private times." She would ask what he had to hide. He would tell her, "Nothing. I just wanted to be alone." And she would not be able to accept that, because, in marriage, there wasn't supposed to be such a thing as "alone." Alone was for bachelors and unmarried women and criminals; marriage was for sharing and knowing and tossing secrets away. He had heard it all before, and he knew precisely what it meant: *I own you.*

He glanced at the framed snapshots in the tall armoire opposite his chair. Those snapshots proved it, he thought. There must have been a hundred of them, taken on vacations and Christmases and Thanksgivings, and one or two just for the hell of it. And he was in a lot of them—nearly half—but always with Marilyn beside him, clinging to him, smiling her big, proprietary smile: *See what I've got?*

He wondered if he despised her.

And if he had ever loved her.

He thought he had. Maybe when they were in high school together and the mere act of touching each other was an awe-inspiring thing, when lovemaking meant *commitment* (it had to), which was all right, because then you got to *do it* all the time and nobody cared. Brett shook his head slowly: God, but those were awful times.

And here he was again, sweating blood and trying to cover it with the toys of his adulthood—his big house, his big car, his business, his insurance policies, his clinging wife. Jesus, what could the child locked deep

inside him—screaming, babbling, tearing him apart—
do with those things?

It took several seconds for the quick laughter from
upstairs to filter into his consciousness. He looked toward the source of the sound, listened. Was that his
son laughing?

He stood, moved slowly out of the room, to the bottom of the stairs. He wished he'd turned on another
light before coming down. This house had always unsettled him a little, even in daylight.

The blond boy in the light-blue jacket appeared only
briefly, first at the top of the stairs, then on the landing. He said nothing. He was not even looking in
Brett's direction.

Brett called, "What are you doing?"

And saw his son appear to the right of where the
boy had been.

"Greg?" Brett said. "What's wrong, Greg?"

Greg stared blankly at his father for a moment,
turned, and went back to his room.

Chapter 21

I love you, Andrea. The words were unnecessary, Brett knew. They were a statement of the obvious. They had no place here, now. If his actions hadn't said he loved her, his words certainly couldn't.

"Go ahead and say it, Brett, if you feel a need to."

He stared confusedly at her. Their lovemaking—the physical act—had ended a half-hour before, yet they still lay naked beside each other. And though the fire in the wood stove had gone out, and sharp patterns of frost were starting on the windows, they needed no blanket for warmth.

"How did you know?" he said.

"That you wanted to say you love me?"

She turned her face toward him, rolled over slightly. He watched her breasts move and thought how sensuous and . . . affectionate that movement was. (He had told her a half-dozen times that her body was perfect—"a tribute to creation," he'd said. Any other time, the remark would have embarrassed him; with Andrea it was truth, naked and unembarrassed truth—like their lovemaking.)

"Yes," he whispered.

She rolled over again, onto her back, focused her eyes on the ceiling. (He hadn't told her why her body so appealed to him—that it seemed a magnificent wedding of all that aroused him, and had aroused him in the past. His years of marriage to Marilyn had obliterated what he now thought of as a juvenile love for huge, basically grotesque breasts. Andrea's breasts were small, well-shaped. When she lay on her back, there was only a slight swelling of flesh remaining at the sides.) "Maybe we're too civilized. We have to say what really doesn't need to be said. And if we don't say it, it means somehow, that we don't feel it." (Her rear end delighted him. He had always been delighted by slightly out-of-proportion rear ends; the chauvinist in him said that a woman's rear end should be slightly larger than her top end. He had read once that ancient man had always found rear ends the most hypnotizing part of woman's anatomy. He thought that was a pretty civilized way to think.) "If I were to refuse, Brett, to say that I love you, you would probably think that I don't, despite——"

"No, Andrea. you're wrong."

"I wish I were. But I'm not."

(And comparisons between Andrea and his mother were impossible to avoid. There was no physical resemblance at all—if there was, he thought, she would not arouse him as much as she did, with that demon *incest* leering at him—but her sensitivity, her caring, her sense of humanity—he recalled the spiders in the sink and the words she'd used, his mother's exact words—were uncannily like his mother's.)

He propped himself up on his elbow, reached out, put his hand on her belly. (He longed to tell her all these things because he thought they were marvelous things and worth sharing but he wondered how well he knew her. what her reaction would be.) "*Do* you love me, Andrea?" he said, and knew immediately his mistake.

A look of sadness came into her eyes. She cupped his face in her hands: "My God, Brett, my God—what she's done to you!"

He pulled away. sat up on the bed, fished around beneath it for his socks. "Andrea, can I ask a favor of you?" He heard the annoyance in his voice.

"Yes."

"Can we forgo discussing her—my wife? I mean . . . ever."

"Is it painful to talk about her, Brett?"

He felt her hand on his shoulder and noted that it seemed to have lost much of its warmth. "It's cold in here, Andrea. Let's get dressed."

"You didn't answer my question, Brett. Is it painful to talk about her?"

He stood suddenly, violently, whirled around to face her. "Please . . ." He saw himself in his mind's eye, saw his quick, unreasoning anger, saw Andrea—this beautiful, sensitive woman who had shown him her love—flinch.

"I'm sorry, Brett. I didn't realize."

He lowered his head as if in apology. "No," he murmured. "No, please don't be sorry. It's me. And it's her. She . . . dirties what we are; do you understand?"

"I think so, Brett; do you?"

He looked up, surprised by the question. And was aware that he couldn't answer it.

Andrea got out of bed, kissed him lightly. "I have to be going." She stepped away from him, glanced about for her clothes.

"Yes," he said. "I'll be ready in a few minutes."

"Alone, Brett." She slipped her bra on, hooked it. "For now, alone."

He knew from her tone, and from her look, that it was not a matter for discussion. Still he said, "Why?"

"It's the way it has to be." A statement of fact. "I'm not asking you to understand, only to accept." She pulled her panties on. "Can you accept that, Brett?"

"I don't know; I don't know why I have to. There's so very little that I know about you." *(Only this, Andrea: If there is a God, He looked down on me and saw what I needed, and sent you.)*

"You know what's important"—she smiled warmly —"and you know that you love me." She picked up her yellow blouse from the foot of the bed, put it on, began buttoning it. "If you want to know more, you need only ask." She touched his face with the tips of her fingers; they were cold. "But we've been together several times, now, and you haven't yet asked——" She let her hand drop. "So, you see, you have already told me what's important and what isn't."

"Where do you live?" he asked, and immediately felt foolish, as if he had committed a *faux pas*. "It's not important," he hurried on. "It's not important."

She slipped into her jeans and gestured toward the cottage's front door. "Out there," she said, "about two miles south. If you weren't looking for the house you'd miss it."

He smiled at the revelation. "How come you never told me? I mean, we're practically . . ." He faltered.

"Neighbors?" she teased.

He put the word in context mentally; it sounded ludicrous. "No," he whispered. "I'm sorry."

She zipped up the jeans. "I'm thirty-two years old, have a bachelor's degree in sociology, was married for five years—no children—both my parents are living, but only one of my grandparents, my maternal grandmother, and I——"

"Andrea, please . . ."

She put her loafers on, then her boots, got her suede coat from the coat-tree. "I am reasonably intelligent, have had a number of not-very-stimulating jobs, am an only child——"

"Andrea . . ."

She shrugged into her coat, went over to him, kissed him lingeringly, until he nudged her away. He looked quizzically at her; her lips were icily cold.

"I'll drive you," he said.

She went to the door, pulled it open, and grinned as if at a private joke. "That's very nice," she said, "but not for everyone's eyes."

And she was gone

Brett looked down at himself. He was astonished to discover that, except for his socks, he was still naked. And his erection was massive.

He listened, heard Andrea's footfalls in the crusty snow grow softer. He looked hurriedly around the room, saw his pants crumpled beneath the bed, ran to them, pulled them on, zipped them up with effort, because of his erection. He ran to the door, yanked it open:

"Andrea!"

Like all the other cottages on this side of the lake, his cottage had been built on a narrow, flat ridge of land flanked by shallow, sloping inclines. The lake was to the east, and the gravel road to the west. Most of the trees had long since been cleared to make way for boats and camping equipment. It was less than a minute's walk from the cottage to the road, and to the west of the road was open land for several hundred feet.

Andrea was nowhere in sight.

"Andrea?" Brett said again, though more softly, resignedly. "Andrea?"

Minutes passed. He became aware, at last, that he was shivering violently. "Andrea?" He heard the pleading in his voice. "I . . ." *Need you!* He looked north, then south.

He went back into the cottage.

Perhaps, he thought desperately, she had left something: an article of clothing, her purse, a handkerchief, something. He looked. She had left nothing. Even her glorious smell had dissipated.

He glanced at the clock: 4:45. Christ, they had been together only an hour and a half! An hour and a half now, an hour two weeks from now, perhaps two hours a week later. Christ, what was that? That was nothing. He needed so very much more.

He picked the clock up, stared at it, watched the tip of the second hand sweep inexorably past the name—

Sessions—and then to 1, 2, 3 . . . He gripped the clock tightly, as if able to crush the metal case in his bare hands.

"Andrea!" he screamed. "Andrea!"

Marilyn's eyes narrowed to slits, as if in caricature of a suspicious woman. It was all so clear, even in the way he mixed his drink (he was taking too long; he never took more than a few seconds), in the way he kept his back to her, in his falsely animated conversation at dinner—clear that he was hiding something from her.

"Brett?" She tried to keep her tone even.

"Yes?" he said. He too, she could hear, was straining for the right tone.

"I was wondering how your day went," she said.

Brett smiled nervously. She knew. Or at least she suspected. He forced himself to relax, in fear that she could see something of his smile even though his back was turned. "It went okay, nothing special."

"I called your office; you weren't there. I called a couple days ago, too, and your secretary had no idea where you were."

"Yes, well, today I went out for a few hours to bid a job. I won it, too." He turned, looked at her. "You know the place; it's over on Aberdeen Street. Great big fieldstone house."

"Uh-huh. When was that?"

"Oh, I don't know, Marilyn." He tried to sound vaguely annoyed. "Between three and five, I guess. Why the third degree?"

"I didn't know that's what I was doing."

"Would you like to see the bid sheet?" He knew he was overplaying his hand now.

"Why would I want to see the bid sheet, Brett? Are you saying I don't believe you?" She joined him at the bar, grinned oddly at him (it made him instantly uncomfortable), and fixed herself a daiquiri. "Of course

I believe you. You've never lied to me about anything. Why should you start now?"

No, Brett realized, she knew nothing of Andrea; she was only guessing. "Of course I've lied to you, Marilyn."

She stifled a gasp. *Go on,* her silence told him. A tiny bead of perspiration appeared on her forehead, at the hairline; he watched it for a moment, fascinated, then turned and added more scotch to his drink. *You're drinking too much.*

"Yes," he continued. "You got me a pair of pajamas, white with blue stripes. Remember? Christmas seventy-six?"

She said nothing.

"I told you how nice they were, how much I liked them." He sipped his drink, grimaced; it was too strong. "Well, I despised them, I really did. It's taken me five years to confess that, but at last I have, and I've gotta tell you, it feels——"

"Don't be an ass, Brett."

"I'm merely responding to your suspicions, Marilyn."

She grinned at him again, and now he was able to define what he had seen in that grin before, what he had seen and—for his own sake, for Greg's sake, for *her* sake—denied: malevolence. And hatred—uncompromising, unlimited hatred—subtle but unmistakable, like the symptoms of a disease in its first few minutes.

"Brett, I have no suspicions." And she turned and left the room.

May 15, 1961

The baby-sitter could see that Evelyn Winter was trying hard to control her temper. The baby-sitter nearly smiled, amused by the woman's self-torment.

"And so, dear," Evelyn Winter continued, "you can understand why that doll has got to be found. She's *lost* without it." She paused, then continued: "Of course, I'm not accusing you of anything, dear. It's just that we *have* looked all over the house." Again a pause. "Well," she went on, her tone suddenly less severe, "if you do find it, you will put it aside, won't you?"

"Yes, I will," said the baby-sitter.

"Good." Mrs. Winter turned, opened the front door. "Have a nice evening, dear." And she left the house.

The baby-sitter reached behind the piles of neatly folded diapers in the child's closet. She put her hand on the doll, clutched it a moment, considering. She withdrew the doll. It was luck, she knew, that Mrs. Winter hadn't found it. If she had, the baby-sitter would be out of a job now. Those burn holes would not be easy to explain. God, but that had been a stupid thing to do! Where had her head been? Was she crazy —really and truly and positively crazy? She could have burned the whole freakin' house down. The doll could have smoldered for hours, just like her uncle's couch had when he'd dropped a cigar down between the cushion and arm. A couple hours later—whoosh! The couch had just about exploded. Same thing could have happened with the doll, even though she'd soaked it with water.(Her uncle had soaked the arm and cushion of the couch with water, too.)

If it wasn't so obvious what kind of burns the holes were, she could say that the child had done it—had put the doll too close to the stove, or had gotten hold of some matches. Something. But the holes had been made by a lit cigarette—that was obvious. There would be no questions, only hurt, accusatory, confused looks, then: "I'm sorry, but your services are no longer required here." And that would be the end of this job, probably the end of her baby-sitting days altogether, because Mrs. Winter would be sure to spread the word: "Watch out for her, she's a firebug."

So, the doll had to be gotten rid of somehow.

Buried? Burned? *(No, no—don't make the same mistake twice!)* Cut up into little pieces and mailed to Cleveland? The baby-sitter giggled.

Something had to be done with it. She couldn't hide it in the house; it would be found, eventually. Found and sent to haunt her. (It was such a repulsive doll—it had an ugly flat face, and scary round eyes. Whoever invented Raggedy Ann dolls had to have been a genuine 24-carat sicky. Jesus, that face could give you nightmares! She was doing the kid a favor by getting rid of it.)

The baby-sitter glanced across the darkened room at the crib. Apparently, the child was sleeping.

Cutting the doll up wasn't a bad idea, the baby-sitter decided. But once she had it cut up, what was she going to do with the pieces? Eat them? Stuff them into her pockets?

She ran some hot water into the kitchen sink, flicked the disposal on. She winced; it was a noisy damned thing. She turned it off, opened the bread box, took out a slice of white bread, shredded it into the disposal, and turned the disposal on again. Yes—she grinned—it was a little quieter.

The large pair of pinking shears she found in Evelyn Winter's sewing room were more than adequate. The doll yielded willingly to them—first the hands, then the feet, then the legs. The pieces she cut were uniformly small, so as not to clog the disposal; *that* would be a disaster. *What's this?* she imagined the repairman saying. *Why, it looks like the pieces of a doll.* The baby-sitter shuddered.

"Dolly!" she heard. She turned her head, confused. She saw darkness beyond the kitchen, little else.

"Dolly!" she heard again, louder.

She looked toward the source of the sound, saw only

darkness. She clutched what remained of the doll in one hand, the scissors in the other; she moved slowly out of the kitchen and into the living room.

She stopped.

"My dolly!" she heard.

And she saw that, somehow, she had forgotten to close the child's bedroom door. It was wide open. And the child, for God's sake, was watching her. Watching her!

The baby-sitter glanced at the doll, then at the small whitish form in the dark adjoining room. She swore beneath her breath at her stupidity.

"My dolly!" she heard again, and saw the small form move slightly. "My dolly, my dolly, my dolly!" The form moved more frantically, and the baby-sitter realized that the child was bouncing up and down in the crib and pointing desperately at the dismembered doll. "My dolly!"

The baby-sitter rushed into the child's room, flicked the light on.

The sudden brightness quieted the child, temporarily. Until she again saw the doll. "My dolly!" she screeched. "My dolly, my——"

"Shut up!" hissed the baby-sitter. "Shut up!"

The child fell silent. She stared wide-eyed, pleadingly, at the doll. Tears started down her cheeks.

"Your dolly is dead." The baby-sitter tried to strike a firm but sympathetic tone, "It got sick and your mommy and daddy said to kill it."

The child looked up from the doll to the baby-sitter. The pleading, wide-eyed disbelief was still on her face, in her eyes.

"Your dolly is dead," the baby-sitter said again. "Your mommy and your daddy——" She stopped, confused, for suddenly, inexplicably—as if resigned to the death of the doll—the child had lain back down.

"Dolly," she whispered. "Dolly." And she was asleep.

Chapter 22

Where would he deliver it? Brett wondered. To what address? And would Andrea understand it?

Dearest Andrea,

I am facing something that I realize now I've refused to face most of my adult life: I'm not a happy man. It's not that I'm unhappy; I'm not—at least not actively so. I don't go around weeping (much, sometimes, as I wish I could). I feel dull. Bored. Except when I'm with you. Jesus, what do I say—thanks for showing me what real happiness is? That's like saying thanks for giving me my life back. Because that's precisely what you've done. I know that sounds corny, but I feel corny. And it feels great.

What do I say about Marilyn? I can't honestly say that our life together has ended, because we never *had* a life together. We live in the same monster house and occasionally we fuck each other. That sounds crass, I know, but our marriage is crass. It's an abomination.

Am I going to leave her? Am I even going to tell her about us? I want to, I ache to, but I've come to realize something else: I'm one of the world's greatest cowards. Because although it *is* an abomination that Marilyn and I have become, it is also something I've grown used to, a kind of security—like the man who's been in prison for twenty years. That prison has become his home, and leaving it would take superhuman courage. That's what I am—a prisoner—and I know it. And it occurs to me just now, as I write, that maybe you haven't done me such a great service after all. Because you've made me realize what I am— the cringing, pathetic *thing* that I am—and I don't know if I have the courage to face it. Because there is such comfort and security in being that thing and not knowing it, in living it day after day after day and thinking, every once in a while, God, but time is really moving by me. Where's it going? Where am *I* going? Do I say thank you for showing me the cripple that I am?

Yes. Thank you. Because now I know why I've been running so fast and getting nowhere.

Brett

He folded the letter neatly and put it in his coat pocket. *About two miles south. If you weren't looking for the house you'd miss it.*

He put the car in gear. Soon he saw his own cottage coming up on the right. He slowed the car slightly; such unbelievably good memories were attached to that little place now. *Sweet to replace the sour,* he thought.

The name *Ferraro* on the old rural mailbox would have escaped him entirely had he not been looking in its direction, fascinated by a motionless white-tailed deer knee-deep in snow near the tree line, about twenty feet from the road.

He brought the car to an abrupt stop. Andrea had said two miles, and he had gone barely a mile. He turned in the seat, looked through the car's rear window, and found that if he squinted, he could dimly see his cottage's roof line not even a half-mile off. So, this driveway was probably not Andrea's; it probably

led to a relative's house, an aunt's or an uncle's.
Around the lake, it wasn't unusual to find members
of the same large family living within a couple miles of
one another.

He was out of the car without thinking, driven by
the impulse to know, to be certain. He pulled the mailbox open, peered in, ran his hand around inside it. It
was empty. "Damn it!" His gaze fell on the long, snow-
covered driveway. He'd never get the car up it, he
knew. And he couldn't even be certain there was a
house at the end of it; he couldn't see one. Only the
new snow (from a recent storm), a small stand of
maples and oaks to the left, a rusted barbed-wire fence
to the right (a faded No Trespassing sign hung from
it), and, still motionless a hundred feet north, the
white-tailed deer.

Brett felt a quick chill.

The deer bolted. In a moment it was gone.

Brett started up the driveway.

I am possessed, he thought. *I am possessed totally.*

His feet had numbed only minutes after he started
up the driveway. He wore no boots, only highly polished black oxfords.

*Possessed, both by Andrea and by Marilyn—Andrea
as my lover, Marilyn as my jailer.*

His tweed coat offered little protection against the
steady, bitter wind that pushed up from the lake (*a
sadistic wind,* he remembered; *a killer wind*). And he
was breathing through his mouth now from the effort
of wading through the deep snow.

Damn my cowardice! It was an easy thing to damn,
he realized; a much harder thing to conquer.

His lungs ached from the cold. The air seemed
slightly rarified here. He glanced about. The driveway
was on a steep incline; the house—which he couldn't
yet see—was apparently near the top of a high ridge
that overlooked the lake.

He wondered, suddenly, if his cowardice doomed him.

The snow, he noticed, was harder and crustier halfway down. He decided that meant something; and wondered what it meant. He shoved his hands into his coat pockets—his soft leather gloves offered no warmth at all. A moment later his foot caught on a particularly hard crust and he fell slowly, almost in the pantomime of a fall, face forward into the snow. He thrust his hands through the several, successively harder layers of snow until he found the surface of the driveway itself, then pushed himself to his feet. "For Christ's sake!" he muttered. He brushed himself off. He saw that a wind-driven snowfall had begun.

Am I doomed to living my life out as a coward, a prisoner? Do I value my security so highly that I'm willing to give my life up to it? He found that he despised his thoughts; they were painful. They could so easily and quickly lead to change, upheaval. And was that fair?

The snowflakes were tiny, pelletlike, and when they hit the exposed area at the back of his neck, they stung. He tried to hitch his coat up so that his neck was protected, but found that it made him lose some of his balance in the layers of snow. He stopped, scanned the hillside. Nothing. Jesus, where *was* this house?

Was it fair to Greg, whom he hardly knew? And even to Marilyn? His mind reeled at that. Did he still have some feeling for her? Was he actually concerned that she might be hurt if he left her? Was his presence in her life required? Did she——

"Goddamnit!" A violent chill went through him as the strong wind bit through his coat. He felt suddenly naked, exposed, mortal.

He looked back at the car. It was barely visible through the gathering storm, and it was at a greater distance than he'd supposed. That comforted him a little;

it also frightened him, because it meant that he was beginning to lose track of himself, was letting his thoughts overwhelm him. And now—at this moment, in this place—that was a stupid and dangerous thing to do.

He plodded forward.

Moments later he saw the house.

Christine sighed and put the brush on the palette. She studied the beginnings of her new painting critically, decisively. At best, she told herself, it was pleasant and amateurish. Most importantly, it did absolutely nothing for her. God, how it annoyed her when she was unable to do truly good work, when the best she could do was this . . . pleasantness. But she was tired. And that was as good an excuse as any.

Tim came up behind her. "Very nice," he said. "I don't think it'll set the art world on fire, but it *is* nice."

She turned a little, took a mock swipe at him with the brush. "You can't tell me," she said, "that there haven't been days when all your camera could focus on was flowers and dirty children and blind beggars."

"Some people make quite a handsome living with that kind of photography, Christine. Don't knock it."

"I'm sure they do."

"In fact, some very eminent——"

"Tim, I'm not up to another artistic discussion. I'd just like to relax and finish this . . . this thing as quickly as possible. Okay?"

"Okay." He made a show of sounding hurt. "I've got some work to do upstairs, anyway." He turned, started for his studio. "Oh," he called, "don't cut off your ear while I'm gone."

"Bastard," she said playfully. She glanced out the window. She felt thankful that the "record-breaking winter storm" had made it necessary for Tim to come home early.

*   *   *

Brett pressed his thumb hard against the doorbell. He listened. He could hear nothing above the sounds of the storm. He stepped back from the door, "Andrea!" he screamed, and noted that his voice sounded weak, ineffectual. "Andrea!" He looked right, then left. The storm obliterated everything ten feet to either side. He could see only that the house was a faded blue in color, two stories tall, a frame house much like what the Hausers had lived in. And something about it—he couldn't quite determine what—disturbed him. Something in the slant of the wall, in the color of the paint.

He stepped back to the door, put his face to it, felt the cold, scarred wood scrape against his cheek. "Andrea," he said, his tone merely conversational. "Andrea, it's me. I need you, Andrea." *You're losing touch, Brett.*

"Andrea, please . . ."

And the door swung open.

Tim picked the brush up from Christine's lap. He cringed a little at the blob of yellow paint on her jeans. She'd be angry with herself for that. She'd say what a stupid and clumsy thing it was to do, that from now on he'd have to keep a close watch over her.

"Tim?" Her eyes fluttered open. She saw the paint smear. "Damn it!"

"It's nothing," Tim said. "If we wash it right away——"

"No. Forget it. Just get me a wet paper towel."

He started for the kitchen.

"Tim," she called, "how long was I asleep?"

"Not long. A half-hour, I guess." And he wondered why he'd lied. What difference was there, really, between a half-hour and an hour? So, she'd fallen asleep for an hour. Her work tired her.

He wet the paper towel, went back to the living room. "Here you go," he said. Christine said nothing.

"Christine?" Still nothing. He went around to the front of the chair. "Honey?"

She was asleep.

Brett lay face down on the faded linoleum. He had caught glimpses, as he fell, of an old refrigerator, and a small stove (the name *Welbilt* flashed through his memory, and he remembered thinking that it was not the inspiration of genius).

"Andrea?" he whispered.

He focused on a worn pattern of random blue and green flecks in the linoleum. *God, that's tacky;* he thought.

"Andrea?" he said again.

He became aware of numbness in his hands and feet. He moved his head a little. His right hand was palm down on the linoleum under his shoulder. That surprised him. He had supposed that his arm was extended, the back of his hand against the floor near the top of his thigh.

He saw the snow piling up around him, felt the wind against the back of his neck, against his cheek. "Hello?" he said, and wondered immediately if he had actually said it. "Hello? Help me, please." He listened to himself. Suddenly pitied himself.

And then it all came together for him: This house had been abandoned. Nothing but spiders and birds and mice lived in it. It waited for the wreckers or time to deliver it.

"Christ . . . oh, Christ!"

COUPLE FOUND DEAD OF EXPOSURE.

He made a weak fist, lifted it, let it drop. "Damn it to hell!"

COUPLE FOUND DEAD OF EXPOSURE.

It had happened nine or ten years earlier—the scandal of the winter. He remembered discussing it with Marilyn, remembered editorializing angrily about the awful insensitivity of the fuel-oil supplier in shutting the old couple off during the coldest month of the year, remembered thinking that Marilyn hadn't seemed to care very much: "It's not really any of our concern, is it, Brett?"

"Goddamnit! Goddamnit!"

And the old couple's name had been Ferraro. Joseph and Marie Ferraro. In their eighties.

Dead of exposure.

In this house.

Ten years ago.

"Andrea?"

Get the fuck hold of yourself, Brett!

With great effort, he pushed himself up on all fours. He turned his head, saw white beyond the kitchen door, nothing else.

"The worst storm of the decade," they'd say. "Came at us right out of Canada." And the news story would read: "Brett Courtney, prosperous 39-year-old insulation contractor, was found dead early yesterday, the victim of exposure. . . ."

He scrambled to his feet and lunged against the door. It slammed shut, and he crumpled with his back to it, his feet and legs alive with pain. He closed his eyes. "Help me," he murmured. "Help me."

"I'm here, Brett."

He opened his eyes, saw the snow piled around him, the stove, the refrigerator.

"In the living room, darling."

He saw a wisp of dark hair appear in the kitchen doorway. "Andrea?" he said.

"In the living room, darling. It's cold. Come get a fire started."

He put his hands on his thighs; he could feel nothing. "Andrea, I can't."

"But you can, my darling. Believe me. You can. I'm cold, too. Come get a fire started."

He squeezed his thighs; some feeling had returned to them. He reached up, grabbed the doorknob. "Yes," he said. He pulled himself to a standing position, gasped at the pain, and, like a drunk, stumbled across the kitchen, through an adjoining hallway, and into what had once been the living room. He stopped, leaned against the archway. "Andrea?"

"I'm here, darling."

He looked toward the source of her voice.

She sat half in darkness in an old overstuffed chair in a far corner of the room. He could see the bottom of her suede coat, her green dress, her calves and feet, the backs of her hands where they rested on the arms of the chair.

"Andrea, darling——"

"The fireplace, Brett."

She pointed. He looked. The fireplace was large and functional; there were beer cans strewn around it, some pieces of waxed paper, a discarded paperback novel.

"Andrea, I don't understand——"

"Hunters use this house from time to time, Brett. They make sure the fireplace is in working order."

"But the firewood——"

"You can use this chair." She stood, stepped away from the chair. "It won't be hard to break apart, Brett. It's very old, and the stuffing will catch easily."

"But——"

He saw her point again. He looked.

"There," she said, "near that book."

He took a deep breath. The numbness was returning. A long sleep seemed quite appealing.

"Near that book," he heard, and was aware that the voice was insistent.

He lurched toward the fireplace, stopped, stood unsteadily over the book, stared at it a moment without comprehension. And saw the box of kitchen matches.

Seconds later he was face down on the floor.

*   *   *

The movements of Christine's hand and arm were quick, almost furious.

"What's that?" Tim asked.

The white paint she was using now had obliterated the still life she'd been working on. The not-yet-dry greens and yellows of the still life blended with the long, slanting strokes of white to produce an effect of vast and frenzied confusion.

"It's a snowstorm, of course," Christine told him. "Any fool can see that."

"Then, I must be a fool," Tim said (*She's just tired*), "because I can see that it's a snowstorm."

"Don't patronize me, Tim."

She put the brush down, picked up another, dipped it into some brown paint. She transferred it to the canvas, worked at it a moment.

"Who's that?"

"It's a man."

"Oh?"

"Yes. He's lost in the storm."

"Will he find his way out of it?"

"I asked you not to patronize me, Tim. I don't know if he'll find his way out of it. It's up to him."

Tim nodded out the window. "Is that the storm you're painting?"

"Yes."

Tim studied the painting a moment longer. "It looks good," he told her. "It looks very good."

"I can *feel* it," she said "You've got to feel it to paint it."

Tim said nothing. The painting wasn't merely good; it was a kind of cold and harsh reality all its own. It disturbed him. It made his pulse quicken, made him dizzy. And afraid.

Brett's first awareness was of warmth against his closed lids—a slightly pulsating, prickly warmth. "Andrea . . ." He barely heard his own voice. "Andrea?"

He opened his eyes. The chair had been sacrificed. The fire was dazzling.

At the periphery of his vision, he saw a pile of clothes. He turned his head slightly; they were his clothes—his coat, his shoes, his pants, even his underwear. "What the——"

"It's okay, fella." A man's voice. "You're gonna be okay. Good thing I spotted your car down there."

Brett turned his head further, saw the old lined face, the friendly gray eyes. "Who are you?"

"Name's Peters, Matt Peters. I'm the deputy sheriff round here, Mr. Courtney."

"How'd you——"

"Had to take those wet clothes off ya, so I checked your ID while I was at it. Few more minutes, you woulda bought the farm for sure, so I figured if there was anyone to notify, I'd have to know who you was." He nodded toward the window. "Musta been all of twenty degrees in here; it's about zero out there. Never seen a blizzard like this, not in all my sixty-three years. Got my jeep stuck halfway up that accursed driveway." He paused briefly, then said, "Ya mind tellin' me what you was doin' here?"

"I thought . . . a friend of mine lived here. A woman."

"No woman here when I got here, Mr. Courtney. And only your tracks, what was left of 'em."

Brett accepted the man's words without question: He wouldn't understand; he couldn't.

"Thank you," Brett said.

"Wasn't nothin'. Just doin' my job, is all."

"Thank you," Brett repeated. And added, "Thank you for more than I can say."

Chapter 23

Sonny Norton had never before felt a pain like the pain that was pushing through him now. It had started in his head, just a whisper of pain, as if some small insect were trying to burrow into his scalp. It had quickly escalated, vaulted into his neck and shoulders, then into his chest and legs, as if some great invisible animal was on him, pushing him to the sidewalk, trying to suffocate him. He groaned, tore at his shirt, his ears, his hands. He fell to his knees, groaned louder, longer.

And the pain was gone. He continued groaning, though only in memory of the pain. He looked about. Marilyn Courtney's house was to his left, Christine Bennet's to his right.

The insect started burrowing into his scalp again. He stood jerkily, panic overcoming him, and stumbled away.

Chapter 24

Brett mixed himself another scotch and water, sipped it. "Something for you?" he said.

"No," Marilyn answered. "Just get on with it."

Brett looked quizzically at her. "What does *that* mean?"

"You've got something you want to talk about. It's been obvious ever since you got home. Jesus, Brett, you think I don't know you after sixteen years? You're predictable; you have routines. Like drinking. You do your drinking after supper. I've never seen you pour a drink at this hour—it's not even time for lunch. There have been other things, too. For instance, you've been talking in your sleep. And you said a name."

Brett stiffened. "A name?"

"Yes. I don't know whose name, but it certainly wasn't mine."

"Well, I don't have any——"

"So, I have to assume that you've got something on your mind. Am I right or wrong?"

Brett hesitated. So, the time had come—sooner than he'd hoped. He'd hoped for a week or two, for time enough to sort things out in his own mind, time enough to somehow ease Marilyn into it, though he had never had any idea how.

"And I know," Marilyn added, "that you didn't go up to the cottage just to get it ready for the summer. You don't do things like that, Brett."

And Brett realized that "time enough" was a rationalization, his cowardice coming back. Time and distance and warmth were weakening him.

"Brett, I'm waiting."

"You're right, Marilyn." A moment after the words escaped him, he wanted desperately to call them back. "You're right," he repeated, because he wanted even more desperately to be certain she heard the words.

She grinned—the same malicious grin he had seen two weeks earlier, only now it had an added dimension: *Gee, this might be entertaining.* "Go on, Brett." She crossed her legs as if making herself comfortable. "Who is she?"

"Her name doesn't matter."

A look of quick and very intense pain flashed across Marilyn's face. Her grin vanished. "It matters, Brett!" She spat the words. "It matters to me."

He downed the rest of his drink. "Andrea," he said. "That's her name—Andrea."

Marilyn's grin reappeared. "Yes, continue."

"And you could say . . . that I loved her."

Silence. Stiff, cold silence. And that damned grin.

Brett poured himself another scotch, stared at it blankly a moment, then dumped it into the ice bucket. "It all started about a month ago." He waited for her to interrupt, but she said nothing. He looked quizzically at her—her silence was beginning to unnerve him —and continued: "We never talked about divorce or marriage or anything like that." He noted the uneasy tone in his voice, noted that it was on the verge of a whine; Jesus, if she'd just stop grinning. "We loved each other, Marilyn; it's as simple as that. We loved each other. Totally." And a simple, hard truth struck him: He had been using the past tense to describe his relationship with Andrea, as if, having come magically into his life, she had magically gone out of it, forever. "And you know, the beautiful thing, Marilyn, the really beautiful thing is, we never said it. We didn't have to say it; we lived it every time we were together." And

it struck him, too, that this truth—that Andrea had
come into his life, had helped him to change it, and
now was gone from it—did not really sadden him,
because, he thought wryly, the beautiful and impossible
fantasy that Andrea was could hardly last very long.
He closed his eyes briefly, suddenly aware that he had
stumbled into yet another truth, but one that was far
more complex, one that his logic told him wasn't at
all possible. "And that feeling Andrea and I had,
Marilyn—that love is so obvious it doesn't need to be
said—is something I've never experienced before."

Marilyn stood abruptly. She was still grinning. Brett
could see that her hands were clenched into fists, her
knuckles white. He thought, *My God, what have I been
saying?*

"I'm sorry, Marilyn, forgive me, I didn't mean——"

She turned and left the room. Brett listened as she
went up the stairs to their bedroom. Listened as she
closed the door. Locked it.

And listened in disbelief to the long, catlike scream
that caromed off the inner walls of the house.

Dear Tim,

I feel tired. I've never felt this tired before. I
wish I could compare it to something you'd recognize. I wish I could say I feel as if I've just run ten
miles.

A comparison does come to mind. I hope you
understand it. First, you must know that this tired-
ness I feel is not a physical thing. Going to sleep
for twenty-four hours would have no effect on it.
Nor is it a mental exhaustion. I think it's mostly
an emotional weariness, as if I've been waiting a
long, long time for some very momentous thing
to happen to me. Like waiting and waiting for an
important letter to arrive, only much more pro-
tracted than that. And I don't know when this
thing will happen, or why, or even what it is,

only that it will happen and that my life will be changed by it. And so I feel in a constant state of transition, as if I'm being taken somewhere by someone for some reason, and though in time I will know all the why's, they are being hidden from me now.

I doubt that I'll give you this letter.

Christine

Brett cringed, remembering his words. He knew now precisely what "twisting the knife" meant. He'd not only twisted it; he'd shoved it in up to his wrist and run it around inside her for a while. Small wonder her reaction.

And yet it had been such an inhuman scream—not just a scream of agony, but grotesque agony, as if she'd been exploding from the inside, and slowly, slowly. As if, in those long, terrible seconds, he was hearing some abominable creature that had crept into the room with her, put its vile hands over her mouth, and screamed for her.

He shuddered and cursed his imagination.

The important thing was, the marriage was over. At last. And that meant readjustment.

He would let her keep the house, of course. It was hers, really. She had decorated it, she had seen to its renovation—the hiring of plumbers and electricians, carpenters and groundsmen—and she so reveled in the product of her labors. And if she were forced to move to some other house, an ordinary house with twelve-by-twelve-foot rooms and coffinlike closets, her claustrophobia would soon overwhelm her.

The queen and her castle. Let her have the house.

Greg, however, was another matter entirely.

He thought, suddenly, that he should have locked the door to this room. Should have closed it, anyway. He sat up in the bed. He felt unaccountably thankful for the yellow night-light in the hallway. He knew instantly, and with a tinge of regret, why he was thankful: Marilyn frightened him. Her grin frightened him, and her silence. He felt comforted that he was in a room on the opposite side of the house from her. He thought that when he actually moved out, his damned migraines would finally go away.

He lay down again. Marilyn was no threat to him. She was a threat to herself, perhaps. But not to him.

In his entire fifteen years in the house, Brett had never slept in this part of it. There were three bedrooms, all off the same long hallway, which were reserved for the occasional overnight guest, usually one of Marilyn's relatives. (Brett's relatives rarely visited. His brother, Lou, had come closest to explaining why: "It's a very nice house, Brett, but the atmosphere's a little stiff, isn't it?" Brett knew what he meant. Marilyn was a big part of the atmosphere of the house.) And because he'd never slept here, he was unaccustomed to the noises the house made on this side. On the other side, a brisk wind could cause the window casings to groan dramatically, and, on particularly humid nights, the house made strange, random, cricketlike noises (it had something to do with the expansion of the wood beneath the new metal siding on the house's back wall, he supposed). The toilet adjoining their bedroom made its own noises, too—persistent, low gurgling noises. ("You got a hell of a lot of plumbing in this house," the plumber explained. "Sure you're going to get some noise from it. Sure.")

Brett listened. The rasping sounds seemed to be coming from the end of the hallway, near what Marilyn called the Red Room (because the motif was predominantly, and loudly, red).

"Marilyn?" he called.

Silence.

He decided in the next moment that if she *was* on her way to this room, the old floor would shout her approach. He imagined her moving slowly, stealthily down the hallway, some kind of weapon in hand, keeping her weight on the extreme right or left side and away from the middle, because that's where the boards creaked loudest, of course. The image made him chuckle nervously.

"Marilyn?" he said again, surprising himself.

He swung his feet to the floor.

He heard the rasping sounds again, closer, near the second bedroom.

He stood, moved on tiptoe to the door, stuck his head out, squinted down the hallway.

"Daddy?"

It was Greg.

"Tim, I wrote you a letter."

Tim rolled to his shoulder. "Oh? When can I see it?"

"I put it in the garbage disposal."

"Why'd you do that?"

"Because I didn't want you to read it."

Tim smiled a nervous smile. Why was she being so cryptic? "If you didn't want me to read it, Christine, you wouldn't have written it."

"Uh-huh. I guess." She nodded out the window at the dark bulk of the Courtney house. "It's very big, isn't it?"

"Christine, the letter . . ."

"A person could easily lose himself in a house that big." She turned her head to look at him. "Do you know, it has fourteen rooms. *And* a semifinished attic. That's what Marilyn told me." She turned back, focused on the house again. "Marilyn's not *all* bad, Tim."

"I never said she was. Besides, I thought we were talking about this letter you wrote, the one you put in the disposal. Don't dangle the bait and then snatch it away."

"That's very colorful, Tim."

He gave her a puzzled look; her remark had been biting, sarcastic. "I'm sorry," he said, for lack of anything else to say.

"No, Tim, *I'm* sorry. I'm just tired. That's what the note was about—about being tired. Emotionally tired."

Tim touched her cheek gently, as if she were very fragile. "Do you want to see your doctor?"

"No," she answered after a moment. "I'm okay. It's something that comes and goes. I'm okay."

"I don't understand."

"I don't either, Tim. I wish I did."

"And what if . . . I were to *order* you to see your doctor?" *God,* he thought, *that sounds foolish.*

Christine said nothing. Her grin mirrored his thoughts.

"Well," he continued, "I don't mean it *that* way. I mean . . . what if I were to ask you, for your own good——"

Her gaze settled again on the Courtney house. "When I think it's time," she said, and Tim noticed something distant and cold in her voice.

"And my opinion doesn't matter?"

She turned her head, touched his face affectionately. "Of course it does." She turned back, studied the house silently a long moment. Then: "It certainly is big, isn't it, Tim. Why would three people want to live in a house that big?"

Tim said, "I don't know, Christine."

Christine said nothing.

Brett seated Greg in a yellow club chair near the bed. "What's the matter, son?" And seated himself on the bed, hunched forward, hands clasped loosely in front of his knees. He was trying to look casual, trying to put Greg at ease. He talked with Greg so rarely— he couldn't remember the last time.

"What are you doing up at this hour, Greg? Isn't tomorrow a school day?"

Greg looked pained by the question, and Brett knew why immediately. He was talking to him the way Marilyn talked to him—in accusations: *Why are you doing this? Why aren't you doing that? Aren't you supposed to be doing something else?*

"Yes," Greg began, "but I——"

"I'm sorry, Greg, forgive me. So what if tomorrow's a school day. I can't tell you how many school days I missed when I was your age, and I made it through." He put his hand reassuringly on top of Greg's. "So tell me, what's troubling you, son?"

Greg looked at his father's hand as if it were something foreign and he wasn't sure what to do with it. Brett withdrew it uneasily. "Tell me what's wrong," he repeated.

Greg glanced tremblingly around the room. Brett could see that he was on the verge of tears. "Is this . . . where you're going to sleep now? You're not sleeping with Mommy anymore?"

Brett paused, considered. Then: "Your mother and I will be living in separate houses from now on, Greg."

"You don't . . ." The tears started. "You don't love each other anymore?"

Brett again put his hand on Greg's. Greg seemed not to notice. "No, we don't, son."

Greg yanked his hand away. He jumped to his feet. "Then, I don't love you, either!" he screeched.

And he ran from the room.

It was seconds before Brett recovered from the shock of that outburst. He ran to the door, looked down the hallway. Greg was nowhere in sight. "Greg?" He listened. After a moment, he heard, faintly, a door slam shut. "Oh, hell," he whispered.

He went back to the bed, lay down, put his hands behind his head. *I'm sorry, Greg. I really am sorry.* And his testicles exploded with pain.

He screamed, doubled up, rolled to the left, away from what had hit him.

"Fucking miserable bastard!" he heard. "Fucking miserable bastard!"

He was hit again, just above his right knee, but because of that other, monstrous pain he barely felt it.

"Fucking miserable bastard!"

He rolled again, thudded to the floor, opened his eyes very briefly. "Marilyn, please . . ." He saw the club head—a 9-iron. "Oh, Jesus!" It stopped, deflected by the mattress, inches from his nose.

He continued to roll, aware all the while of his screams, aware, also, that he was trying to form Marilyn's name and couldn't, aware that she was rounding the bed, was standing over him, was bringing that 9-iron high over her head. . . .

"You want to know why Daddy's leaving us, Greg? You want to know why?"

"Mommy, I heard someone screaming. Who was it?"

"Daddy's leaving us, darling, because he doesn't like us anymore. He won't tell me why he doesn't like us; he just says he likes somebody else a lot better. Do you understand?"

"It sounded like somebody was hurt real bad, Mommy. Didn't you hear?"

"Greg, listen to your mother. Don't interrupt. Daddy's going to be living somewhere else. You and I are going to live here alone. Do you think you'll like that?"

"But——"

"I asked you a question, Gregory. Answer it. Don't you think you'll like living here alone with me? Won't that be fun?"

"Yes."

"Yes what, Greg?"

"Yes it'll be fun."

"That's better. Okay, darling, get out of bed."

"But it's not time to——"

"Don't *argue* with me; just do as I tell you. Get *out* of the bed."

"Yes, Mommy."

"Good. We're going to play a game."

"Mommy, I'm real tired——"

"I didn't ask if you were tired, did I? I told you we were going to play a game."

"Yes, Mommy."

"That's a good boy. Now, put your slippers on."

With Brett's return to consciousness came one damnable memory. He'd read it somewhere: Massive injury to the testicles causes pain that never entirely dissipates.

He opened his eyes slowly. And discovered that he had to make his breathing shallow; otherwise the pain was unbearable. "Oh, good Christ——" He clamped his mouth shut. If Marilyn heard him . . .

Could he stand? It amazed him that he was still in a fetal position, hands cupped tightly around his testicles. He made an effort to keep his mind off his hands, for fear they would tell him of some enormous, grotesque swelling. Instead, he concentrated on the pain. He had never before felt anything like it, and it awed him, terrified him. It was, very simply, a pain to which unconsciousness, even death, might be preferable.

But there was Greg to consider. That fact, his awareness of it, let him sublimate the pain momentarily. "Greg," he whispered.

A minute later he was on his feet.

He wanted desperately to silence his rhythmic, low groans, but they were involuntary, as if the pain were sending its own, uncontrollable impulses to his vocal cords.

His hands were still between his legs. He was relieved and astonished to find that he could stand. He wondered if he could make it all the way to the door; it seemed literally miles off, in another world altogether. He took a step. His knees buckled slightly. He halted. Waited. Bent over a little more to ease the pain. He took another step. And another. He thought what a fool he was, how clownish and idiotic he must look. . . .

"What do you think, Greg? Do you think you'll like it in here? It's much bigger, and I'll get you your own TV."

"It's nice, Mommy, but it's cold."

"That's only because the radiator isn't working right. Tomorrow I'll call the radiator repairman and he'll come down and get it working again."

"Do I *have* to stay in here, Mommy?"

"Only as a favor to me, Greg. Only because I want you to. Just think of it as camping out. You like to camp out, don't you? Remember when we used to go to the cottage?"

"What cottage?"

"The one at the lake. You remember it."

"I . . . think so."

"Sure you do, darling. Just make believe that's where you are now. At the cottage. And there's a big storm wailing away outside, but you're all good and snug inside. Isn't that a nice thought?"

"I guess so."

"Sure it is. Okay, get into bed. I'll tuck you in."

Brett pushed the door open. "Greg?"

Silence.

He hobbled into the room, flicked the light on. "Greg?" And saw that the bed, though mussed, was empty. "Greg?" He glanced around the room. "Where are you, Greg?"

And realized the truth: Marilyn had hidden him.

"Shit!"

Pain shot through him. He fell to his knees, grasped his testicles.

"Shit—oh, shit!"

He tried to steady his breathing. The pain ebbed slightly. He reached out, put his hand on a bedpost, let his eyes open.

He saw the gleam of the 9-iron first, then Marilyn's hand resting on the grip. She lifted the club slightly, in the direction of his testicles. She grinned. "I guess you won't be using those again real soon, will you, Brett darling."

He took an aching step toward the doorway.

She raised the club higher. "Stop right there, Brett, or I really will hit you."

Brett stopped. "Where is my son?"

"*Your* son, is it? *Your* son? I *did* have something to do with him, Brett. Don't you remember? Or were you off with some whore!"

"Marilyn, this is pointless——"

She jabbed at his stomach with the club. "I want you out of here tonight, Brett. Tonight! Is that clear?"

"Tell me where Greg is, Marilyn. He's coming with me."

Marilyn threw her head back and laughed. Brett watched incredulously. How could he have lived with this woman all these years and never seen this side of her? Or had he seen it and denied it? Part of his cowardice.

"You're leaving this house alone, Brett. Alone! And don't try any legal maneuvers. It's your word against mine, and the courts still favor the mother. And another thing"—she jabbed at him again; he grabbed for the club, but she withdrew it quickly—"when it *does* come to a court battle, remember it was you who did the cheating, not me. You! I've got proof." She stepped to one side. "I've packed a bag for you. You've got everything you'll need."

He hobbled past her and into the hallway, turned toward the bedroom. "You can't possibly win, Marilyn."

He felt the club head being pushed hard into his spine. "I already have, Brett darling. Hearing your screams, watching you double up, seeing you experience the agony I experienced is victory enough."

"Then, you'll let me have Greg?"

She jabbed harder. He started walking. "Greg is mine, Brett. This house is mine. *You* are shit!"

"Christine, I want you to hear me." Tim waited nervously. This wasn't the first time Christine had broken down and cried without apparent reason, but it had been happening with disturbing frequency ever since their move to the house. "Christine, please . . ."

"I'm . . . confused, Tim. I . . ." She looked up at him. He saw the confusion; it was clear around her eyes and in the line of her mouth, even in the way her head cocked slightly to the right. She winced. "The pain . . ."

Tim leaned over, put his hand under her chin. "Where?"

She smiled pathetically. "Not that kind of pain. It's something else, Tim. I can't explain it." She lowered her head and shook it slowly.

"Do you want to see Dr. Tichell, Christine?"

She shook her head more sharply. "It's not necessary, Tim. I've had these . . . spells before. It's okay. I think it's just the change of scene."

"And what if I *want* you to see the doctor?"

She looked up again. The confusion was leaving her, and the pain. "We've been through all that before, Tim. Please don't press it."

He straightened, put his hands on his hips, tried to bring the heavy sound of authority to his voice: "In some things, Christine——"

She laughed at him, not maliciously, but as if he would naturally share the joke with her—the joke his strained machismo had created. "Tim . . ." was all she could manage through her laughter.

Tim smiled, easily convincing himself that laughter was a far, far better thing than tears, even if his foolishness was the reason for it, and easily forgetting that her tears had ended, much too abruptly, only moments before—and that there was something very odd in that.

June 5, 1961

It was the kind of persistent screech—"Mith King, Mith King!"—that quickly got the baby-sitter on edge. *I want!* it said; *I want, I want, I want!* And it had very nearly the same effect as chalk scraped on a blackboard: The short hairs on the back of the baby-sitter's neck stood on end, and she cringed. "Stop it!" she screamed. The pitch and volume of her voice shocked her. She felt a sharp, stinging pain at the back of her throat. She cringed again, from the pain. "Goddamnit!"

She became aware of the silence. She smiled a tentative, cautiously optimistic smile. It was possible that within minutes the child would start again; she had done it before.

The baby-sitter waited, listened. The silence continued. Good. She had trained the child well. Children were like dogs, really: Just a few harsh words kept them nicely in line.

Now she could make her phone calls.

She picked up the receiver, dialed, waited three rings.

"Hello?" she heard.

She paused a moment, then: "Is this the Vanderburg residence?"

"Yes. Who's calling, please?"

"Is this Mrs. Vanderburg?"

"Yes, it is. May I please ask who's calling?"

"Do you have a daughter named Joanne?"

"Yes, I do. Now, I must insist——"

"This is Mrs. Seaton at St. Mary's Hospital."

"Oh, my God!"

"I'm afraid, Mrs. Vanderburg, that——"

"My God, my God!"

"I'm afraid there's been an automobile accident, and your daughter——"

"Nooooooo!" It was a pleading, senseless wail strung out to several seconds. "Noooooo!"

"Mrs. Vanderburg, please——"

"Is she hurt? Is she . . . Oh, my God!"

The baby-sitter suppressed a giggle. She hadn't realized what a fine actress she was. The woman was really convinced. Well, all these weeks she had probably suspected that *something* was going to happen. Everyone knew what a maniac Bill Williams was; he had already had two accidents. Only his father's influence had stopped his license from being taken away.

"I'm afraid, Mrs. Vanderburg, that the outlook for your daughter is not good. Could you come to the hospital right away?"

There was no reply. Had the woman caught on? Had she—the baby-sitter—betrayed herself somehow? Had her professional tone slipped just enough?

"Noooooo!" she heard. Then the receiver being slammed onto its rest. A dial tone.

The baby-sitter giggled. There was no mistaking that last wail: The woman was convinced. At that very moment she was probably bustling about, tripping over things, babbling, looking for her coat and boots. Crying, too. Lots of great big tears for poor baby Joanne.

And when she found out that her precious daughter was okay, that the supposed accident had only been a joke, she would remember the pain she was feeling now. Remember it and realize that, yes, it could happen, because Bill Williams was a maniac, everyone knew it, and *Joanne, you little brat, if you ever see him again* . . . It was absolutely, positively perfect.

She looked up a number in the phone book, dialed it. A woman answered.

"Is this the Williams residence?" the baby-sitter said.

"Yes."

"Is this Mrs. Williams?"

"This is Ida Williams."

Ida, for Christ's sake. *Ida!* "Mrs. Williams, this is Mrs. Seaton at St. Mary's Hospital."

"Yes?"

The baby-sitter stiffened. No anxiety? Just a simple *Yes?* Joanne Vanderburg and Bill Williams *had* gone out together tonight. she was sure; she had overheard them planning it. Besides, they'd been going out every Friday night, now, for a month.

"Mrs. Seaton?" coaxed Ida Williams.

"Uh——"

"Has something happened, Mrs. Seaton?"

The baby-sitter nearly sighed in relief. It wasn't that they hadn't gone out tonight; it was just that Bill's mother was one of those calm, cool, collected types.

"I'm afraid there's been an accident, Mrs. Williams."

"An accident?" Still calm, still collected. *Not for long, lady.*

"An automobile accident. Your son's been——"

"Mith Kiiinnnggg!"

The baby-sitter turned her head sharply toward the child's room.

Ida Williams insisted, "Who *is* this?"

"Mith Kiiinnnggg!"

The baby-sitter threw the receiver down. "Stop it!" she screamed, and felt the pain again in her throat. She ran to the child's room, to the crib, raised her arm, opened her hand. And heard, very, very faintly, from the living room, "Who *is* this? Who *is* this?"

The child was whimpering in a corner of the crib. "Mith King," she managed, "I'm thorry."

The baby-sitter turned, started out of the room.

"Hello? Miss King, Mrs. Seaton, who*ever* you are! What kind of prank is this?"

The bedroom door slammed shut. The baby-sitter found herself in darkness.

"What the ——" She felt a clammy sweat starting. "Oh, Jesus!" She knew immediately that the walls were only inches from her hands.

And the door was open. Instantly. "I'm thorry, Mith King." As if it had not been shut at all.

The baby-sitter stared for a moment, uncomprehending.

She hurried to the phone, picked up the receiver— "This is really stupid, Miss King; it's cruel, unforgivably cruel"—and put it gently on its rest.

Part Two

GREG

Chapter 25

Greg remembered something about this room, something from years before, and the memory—still amorphous, still only a nebulous, bad feeling—had to do with his father and mother.

He disliked the room. It was too big, and it smelled of dust and age. (his grandmother smelled that way, he remembered, but hers was really a different smell, a nicer smell). And the bedsheets and blankets were stiff and cool, which, he supposed, would have been all right if the room hadn't been so cold. But it *was* cold. It faced the wind and its radiator was on the fritz, so it was cold. He was glad his mother had brought him his coat and gloves.

He wondered when she'd come back. And why, exactly, she'd locked the door. She hadn't told him she was going to lock it. She'd delivered the coat and gloves, said "I'll see you later," and left. Then she'd locked the door.

("It's either this, Brett, or . . .")

The memory made Greg wince. It had to do with that other night his mother had put him in here, that night so long ago that he remembered looking up at her from just above the level of her waist. The image frightened him. He fought it down and busied himself with an examination of the room.

Because it faced north, the room never got any direct sunlight. He thought about putting his little Norfolk Island pine in here and decided it would die in no time. He thought about listening to his record player in here and decided the music would sound hollow, because the room was so big.

"You're selfish, Brett. You're greedy!"

"Why? Because we may have to move out of this monstrosity you call a house and into something a little more reasonable?"

"It's your damned ego that's going to make us move out of here!"

Greg listened to the words playing back; he thought how clear they were, as if they'd been said only minutes before.

And he hated them. They wrapped up something nasty, something that hurt. Which was why, he knew, he hated this room. Because this is where he had listened to those words.

He sat dolefully in a big brown leather chair. Why had she locked the door? he wondered again. When would she unlock it? He glanced about. He felt tears starting and fought them back. He was getting a little too old for tears.

Becky Foster stepped back as Christine pushed the door open. "Morning, neighbor," Becky said. "Nice morning, wouldn't you say?"

"Good morning," Christine said.

Becky noticed something—impatience?—in her tone. Undaunted, she went on: "I was hoping you could do a little shopping with me. Window-shopping, actually. Who has money to shop with, right? But it's a way to get you out of the house. What do you say?"

"Thanks, Becky, but I can't. Marilyn called a little while ago——"

Stiffly: "Marilyn Courtney?"

"Yes. She said she needed to talk to someone."

"You're pretty tight with her, huh?" Becky regretted the words immediately. "No, I'm sorry, Christine. Forgive me."

"It's okay, Becky." (Becky could tell that it wasn't.) "No, we're not . . . tight. She just needed someone to talk to and I was elected. Maybe we can go shopping another day."

"Sure, okay," Becky said, backing down the porch. She turned, started for her house, waved back. "Some other day," she called.

Christine closed the door.

"I thought I knew him." Marilyn leaned forward a little in her chair. "Are you sure you're comfortable, Christine? It must take a long time to get used to that thing." She nodded at the wheelchair.

"Yes," Christine answered. "I'm fine."

Marilyn sat back, held her cup of tea near her mouth as she spoke: "Because, when you live with a person, you assume that you know him, especially after sixteen years." She sipped the tea delicately. "That's how long we were married. Did you know that?"

"No, I didn't."

"Sixteen years," Marilyn repeated. "A long, long time to be deceived, though, of course, I didn't know I was being deceived until yesterday, when he finally confessed his little escapades. It seems he's been whoring around for quite some time. He didn't say exactly how long, but he didn't need to. It's been years, literally years." She set her cup of tea on an end table. "He even said he was going to take Greg away from me." She shook her head slowly, in disbelief. "I told him that it would be impossible, that even if he denied his affairs—which would come down to his word against mine—I've got proof: concrete proof." She paused dramatically. "I was packing a bag for him and I found these." She withdrew several sheets of paper from the pocket of her housedress, waved them around, then put them back in her pocket. Saw the puzzlement on Christine's face. "They're notes, Christine—notes from him to his latest ladylove. Her name's Andrea; he told me that. There are no names on the notes, of course—he's too smart for that—but the handwriting is unmistakably his." She grinned victoriously. "Let the bastard try and take Greg away."

"You helped make him, so now you owe him. And you owe me!"
"That's fucking pathetic, Marilyn."
"Listen, buddy boy, it wasn't you who went through all that goddamned pain, and it wasn't you who cleaned up his crap when it was all over the crib, and it wasn't you who had to give him his goddamned bottle in the middle of the goddamned night. . . ."

With great effort, Greg shut the memory off. He let the tears come.

"You know where it all happened, Christine?"
"No. Tell me." Christine heard the eagerness in her voice; it surprised her.
"It happened at our cottage on Canandaigua Lake. Do you know where that is—Canandaigua Lake, I mean?"
"I think so."
"I've got it all right here." She patted the pocket of her housedress. " 'The cottage. At four,' one of the notes says. That's all—just 'The cottage. At four.' Why he didn't get rid of these notes, I'll never understand. Maybe he *wanted* to be caught. Do you think that's possible, Christine?" It was a rhetorical question; Christine didn't answer it. Marilyn picked up her cup of tea. "I never really needed him, you know. As long as he makes the proper support payments, Greg and I can be very happy here together."

Christine wheeled her chair forward a few inches and cocked her head to one side. "Is that crying I hear, Marilyn? It sounds like someone's crying."

Marilyn rolled her eyes as if in exasperation. "That boy!" She sipped her tea, dabbed at her lips with a napkin. "He's being punished. He said a word I do not approve of, so I sent him to his room. I've tried to break him of that infantile crying habit again and again, but he persists. He's extremely bullheaded, but then, so was I when I was his age."

Greg hated his tears as much as he hated the room, as much as he hated the memories that seemed to flow from the walls of the room. He tried hard to quiet his sobbing: *Baby!* he called himself, but it didn't work.

He rolled over, tried to bury his face in the pillow, hoping that would snuff out the tears. He soon found that he couldn't breathe. He lifted his head.

And realized the truth, at last: He would let her do whatever she wanted to do. She was his mother. She had raised him. She fed him, protected him. He would wander blindly into traffic without her. He was helpless without her.

She was his mother! And that was something almost holy. If she wanted to shut him in this room without food or water or warmth, he would let her.

It was her right.

"What word did he say, Marilyn?"

Marilyn looked confused by the question. She thought a moment, remembered. "It's a four-letter word for intercourse. You know the word."

"Yes, I do."

"So, naturally, I had to punish him. I sent him to his room. He'll stay there for a while." She paused. "Brett would have encouraged him in such language, I'm sure. He would have called it manly. Well, he'll no longer be able to exercise his vile, corrupting——"

The scream surprised them both. Marilyn jumped to her feet, a quivering, nervous smile on her lips. "Excuse me, Christine." She started out of the room. "I won't be long."

"Yes," Christine said. "Take your time."

Greg had heard himself scream and had been disgusted by it, shocked by it, strangely relieved by it—as if something somewhere inside him, some small, self-protective creature that rarely showed itself, had decided that things had gone too far. He would let her shut him up in this awful room, okay—but not without some kind of protest.

But now, the creature had retreated, and Greg's relief was quickly being replaced by a deep and aching embarrassment. Whatever she did to him now, he deserved. If she wanted to whip him with six feet of barbed wire, it would not be too big a punishment for his stupid, stupid scream. . . . But maybe she would think of something else—something not quite so painful as barbed wire.

Marilyn unlocked the door with one quick movement. She pushed it open sharply and glared at Greg sitting on the edge of the bed. "I have company," she said. "Mrs. Bennet from next door. And she's a very, very sensitive woman. You've seen her. She's a cripple. In a wheelchair. And when she heard you scream, she started crying from the shock. Do you want to make her cry?"

She waited. Greg said nothing. His lower lip quivered.

"I repeat, do you *want* to make her cry?"

"No."

"She said what a nice boy she thinks you are. Let's not prove her wrong."

Marilyn left the room and locked the door behind her.

Greg screamed again. Mentally. Loud and long. The

effort threw him against the door. He crumpled there, sobbing.

At least she hadn't used barbed wire.

"Is he okay?" Christine asked.

Marilyn returned to her wing chair. She crossed her legs, pulled her housedress over her knees, smiled apologetically. "He's okay. A nightmare—he had a nightmare." She glanced at her cup on the end table. "Some more tea, Christine?"

"No, thank you, Marilyn. I should be going. Tim will be home soon."

Marilyn stood to escort Christine to the door. "May I?" She indicated the chair's push bars.

Christine smiled. "Of course."

Marilyn pushed her slowly from the room. She stopped in the hallway. "You know, Christine, our little talk has been quite therapeutic for me."

"It was my pleasure, Marilyn. Anytime."

"Can I take that as a promise?"

"Yes—please do."

"Because, as you can imagine—and regardless of the bastard he turned out to be—it's going to get a little lonely here without Brett. This is quite a large house——"

"I've noticed."

"And Greg certainly isn't . . . well, adult companionship. It would be nice if you and I could be friends."

"Yes, that would be nice, Marilyn."

"I don't have many friends, you know."

"I wouldn't have guessed."

"Lots of opportunities, naturally, but very few real friends. I've never had the time for them. Or the patience. People can be such idiots."

"Yes, they can."

"But I like you, Christine. I like you very much."

Christine turned her head and smiled warmly.

"Thank you, Marilyn." She turned her head back. "Tim must be sending the dogs out for me by now."

"Oh, yes. Forgive me."

She pushed Christine briskly to the side door. There was only one, short step down to it, and with Marilyn's help, Christine negotiated it easily. Marilyn opened the door, held it:

"Maybe I could get an estimate on a small ramp, Christine—something like what you've got at your front door."

Christine turned her chair around to face her. She reached out, touched her hand. "Thank you, Marilyn, but it's not necessary. That step's not bad." She withdrew her hand, started down the driveway.

"Be careful," Marilyn called after her.

Chapter 26

"How does this place look?" Marilyn said.

Christine addressed Marilyn's reflection in the shop window: "Expensive."

"It's my treat today, Christine." Marilyn's reflection smiled generously. "A hat, gloves, whatever—it's my treat."

"Marilyn, that's awfully nice, but——"

"And another day it can be your treat."

Christine thought a moment. "Okay," she said. "But nothing too expensive."

Marilyn wheeled her into the shop. A clerk came forward. Marilyn said, "This is my friend, Christine Bennet."

The clerk—a tall, thin, middle-aged woman—nodded and smiled solicitously.

"And since today is her birthday," Marilyn went on, "I'm giving her her pick of anything in the store."

"Marilyn, my birthday's not for eight months."

"That means it's only four months past."

Christine laughed. "That's one way of looking at it."

"Anything," Marilyn repeated. "I'm feeling quite generous."

The clerk gestured toward a display case nearby, "Perhaps some jewelry?"

Christine studied the case a moment. "No, I'm not much for jewelry."

"I have it," Marilyn announced. She turned Christine's chair around, started for the door. She looked back at the clerk. "I'm sorry, dear, but this place is awfully stuffy." She laughed. Then, to Christine: "I just remembered, there's this little art supply shop only a block down the street . . ."

Pain shot through Brett's testicles. He winced, doubled over. The pain slowly dissipated. He breathed long, slow breaths. "She didn't hit them straight on, apparently," he remembered the doctor telling him. "If she had—this is going to be hard to believe, but it's true—if she *had* hit them straight on, the pain would have been even more intense. As it is, you'll probably have occasional pain in the area for several months, perhaps longer."

Brett put his hand against the wall, expecting another attack of pain. He waited. There was a burning sensation in his lower abdomen, but it finished quickly. He continued moving down the hallway toward what had been Greg's bedroom. "Greg?" It was possible, though not likely, that she had put him back in it— because he'd complained about a strange room. She couldn't stand it when he complained; she called it whining. He remembered the time Greg had broken a toe and kept it from them both for a week, not wanting to be scolded for complaining about it.

That was the kind of boy she had turned him into —a scared little boy. Scared to go outside without her permission, scared to play without her permission, scared to do much of anything without her permission, or without, at least, the knowledge that she didn't object. He wasn't the classic "mama's boy": That phrase indicated something that had never existed between Marilyn and Greg—love (even the possessive, cloyingly sweet love that Brett had experienced with his own mother). Marilyn loved Greg no more than she loved her Queen Anne chair or her Duncan Phyfe table. She possessed them; she possessed Greg. And, though it was a damnable and shameful truth, she had possessed him—Brett.

"Greg?" he called. He leaned against Greg's bedroom door, turned the knob. "Greg, are you in there?" He pushed on the door. It swung open.

The room was empty. No bed. No dresser or lamps or bookcase. Just bare walls and bare floor. The aura of hurried abandonment was heavy in the air.

"Goddamnit!" The word came quickly, hollowly back at him and reinforced his sudden anger. He slammed his fist hard into the wall above the light switch. He heard plaster inside the wall crack and fall.

"Goddamnit, Marilyn, goddamnit! You don't have the right, you don't have the fucking right——"

He turned, stepped out of the room, slammed the door shut.

And headed for what had once been his and Marilyn's bedroom.

"This is the first time I've been in here, Christine," Marilyn said quietly, as if she might offend someone with what she was saying. "Though I never really had the need. I adore art, certainly—you know that; you've been in my house—but as far as creating it . . ."

"It's my first time, too," Christine told her, grinning conspiratorially.

"Good," Marilyn said, still quietly. "That makes me feel better." She glanced around. "It's awfully close in here, isn't it?"

"It's a little small; most art stores are."

"Never mind. You pick out something, anything: a new set of paints—what do you use, oil paints?—an easel, a canvas, anything."

"Marilyn, are you sure about this?"

"Of course." She paused, glanced around again. Then, as if to herself: "Almost scandalously small. How's a person supposed to make his way around, for God's sake?"

Christine reached for Marilyn's hand. "Marilyn, are you all right? Do you want to leave?"

"I'm okay," Marilyn answered hesitantly. "I have this little problem——"

"Claustrophobia?"

Marilyn stiffened visibly. "No," she snapped. "Of course not. It's nothing like that at all. Not at all." She paused, breathed deeply. Then: "Anything, Christine. Anything. My treat."

"Let's go, Marilyn. You look uncomfortable."

"I said anything. Do I have to pick it out for you?"

Despite herself, Christine smiled—perhaps, she thought, to help put Marilyn at ease. "Okay, Marilyn, a small canvas, nine by eleven. I need one."

"Nine by eleven?"

"Yes, I can stretch it myself."

"I don't understand."

Christine withdrew her hand and motioned to a clerk nearby. "Just give me a moment."

"Yes, ma'am?" the clerk said.

"Could you tell us where your canvases are, please?"

"Us?"

"My friend and me." She gestured behind her, turned her head slightly.

Marilyn was gone. Christine turned her head further, saw her just outside the door. Marilyn's back was to it. She was shivering violently.

Brett doubled over. He fell to his knees. Waited. Eventually, the pain faded. He stood, cursed himself, though gently. He'd have to watch his temper; it seemed to have a lot to do with the onrush of pain, and if he was going to double over every five minutes because a room he looked into happened not to contain Greg, then he'd be here a long, long time.

A whisper of pain lingered in his lower abdomen. He took a step, felt the pain widen, as if it had been a needle and now was a small nail. He lowered himself to a sitting position in the hallway, chanced a long, slow, deep breath. The pain vanished. "Thank God," he murmured.

He stood. "Greg?" he called. He looked right, then left, unsure of where he had just been. On impulse, he turned left. The attic stairway was ahead, at the end of the hall, and, before that, two rooms he hadn't yet checked. "Greg, please answer me," he called. "Please . . . It's me, your father." He waited. There was no response. "Greg?" Again nothing. He wondered idly if she'd taken him out of the house altogether.

He tried a door. Unlike the others, it was locked. And the lock was new—a Yale lock. *This is it,* he told himself. He put his face sideways to the door. "Greg," he said aloud, comfortingly. "Open the door, son." He put his ear to the door. "Greg?" He listened. Was that Greg breathing just on the other side of the door? "Greg, I've come for you. If you're afraid, don't be. Especially not of me. I love you, son." He stopped, listened again. Had the breathing grown louder, faster? "Greg, open the door." He heard movement inside the room—slight, shuffling sounds, as if someone were stepping slowly and quietly back from the door.

Marilyn's long silence ended when they turned onto Aberdeen Street. "Did you get your canvas?" She looked briefly at Christine. "No, of course you didn't. I was the one who was going to buy it for you, wasn't I."

Christine said nothing. She still wore the smile that had come to her lips when she first realized Marilyn's discomfort in the art store. The smile unsettled her, because she knew now that it had not been intended as a comforting thing at all. It was an amused smile. Marilyn's discomfort—her pain—was amusing. But that was impossible, insane. No one's pain amused her, especially the pain of this woman who was so rapidly becoming her friend.

Marilyn said (as if it were the first time she'd used the phrase with Christine), "It was awfully close in there."

Christine forced her smile down. "Yes, it was. Art stores are usually not very big."

"That clerk was abysmally rude."

"Uh-huh," Christine said.

"You don't think she was rude coming out onto the street and fawning all over me like that? You don't think that was embarrassing?"

"She thought you were in some kind of trouble, Marilyn."

"If I'd been in trouble, I'd have called for help." She turned onto Longview Terrace. "I'll drop you off, Christine, and then I've got to get home and check up on Greg."

"How's his fever?"

"Still up."

Two entities fought for control of Greg. One told him, *It's okay. He's your father and he's never hurt you.* And the other—stronger, louder—kept repeating Marilyn's words: "Greg, if your father comes here looking for you when I'm not home, you're to stay quiet. You're not to utter a peep, not a peep, do you hear? Because if I discover that he's taken you, I'll hold you responsible, and when I find you, by God, I'll——" And then she had smiled—a smile that made him shudder. She had told him other things, things about his father wanting to send him to reform school. He wasn't sure that it was true, but it probably was; his mother said it was. And she had told him that his father had never been a real father to him, had never taken him anywhere—fishing, to the movies, to an amusement park. Other fathers did that, he knew; he had heard the kids at school talking about it from time to time.

"Stand away from the door, son. I'm going to try to break it down."

His father had always been too busy, she'd said: "He liked his work more than he liked you, Greg. Now he likes this other woman more than he likes either of us."

"Greg, are you away from the door?"

It was all probably true, Greg thought now. But that smile! She had used it on him several times before, and he remembered that soon afterward—because, in one way or another, he had displeased her—he had hurt. Bad.

"I'm going to try to break it down now, Greg. Stand away from the door."

No! Greg wanted to cry out. *No!*

He heard a heavy, muffled thud. He saw the door shiver.

"No, Daddy, please don't. Mommy said——"

"Greg? Are you okay, Greg? Stand back. I'm going to try it again."

"No, Daddy!"

Brett hit the door again. The top hinge burst free of the jamb. He hit it once more, with the heel of his foot. The door fell wide open, leaning at a steep angle on its one, bottom hinge.

Greg stared a moment at his father, saw him hold his hands out.

"It's okay." Brett got down on his haunches. "It's okay, son."

Greg's eyes widened. Brett saw, confusedly, that he was apparently focusing on something in the hallway behind him.

"Greg, what's the matter?"

"Mommy, don't! Mommy, please!"

Brett turned his head quickly, saw the glint of the raised club head. "Oh, Jesus!" Saw the impossible, animal grin on his wife's face, heard her high screech —"Bastard!"

He rolled to his right, saw the club head hit the floor where his head had been just a second before, heard a grunt come from him, found himself scrambling to his feet, saw the club head being raised high once more, heard the pleading, disbelieving voice of his son— "Mommy, don't!"—saw the club head coming down, felt a slice of pain near his left temple. . . .

Chapter 27

Becky Foster's manner disturbed Christine; it was almost proprietary. *I found you first,* it told her, *and Marilyn Courtney's not going to butt in.*

Becky went straight to the kitchen, started some coffee. "Let's talk," she called.

Christine wheeled herself from the living room to the kitchen doorway. "Sure. What about?"

"About friendships."

"Anyone's in particular?"

"Uh-huh. Ours." She got some cups and saucers out of a cupboard, set them on the counter. "Cream, no sugar—right?"

"Right."

"You don't mind if I help myself to your kitchen, do you?"

"I don't mind." Christine noticed a coolness in her tone and regretted it. "Of course I don't mind." She paused. Then: "You were saying, Becky, about friendships . . ."

"Actually, I wanted to talk about the responsibilities of one friend to another."

"Yes?"

"My responsibility to you, to be precise."

"Yes?" Christine repeated.

The coffee was ready. Becky poured two cups, handed one to Christine. They went into the living room. Christine wheeled herself to the window that overlooked the Courtney house. Becky sat in the wicker chair across the small room.

"I wanted to tell you, Christine, that Marilyn Courtney is using you. I wanted to tell you that I don't like it."

Christine sipped her coffee. She wondered what expression she was wearing—annoyance? pleasure? Or was she merely blank? She had guessed, in substance, what Becky was going to say, but now that it had been said, she had no idea how she felt about it. "Go on, Becky."

"And I can't believe you don't *know* she's using you."

"That's a pretty loaded statement, Becky. If she were using me, would I continue the friendship?"

Becky thought a moment. Then: "I don't know," she answered. "Would you?"

"What's *that* supposed to mean?"

Becky looked suddenly, genuinely confused. "Damn it!" To herself. At herself. "I have no idea, Christine. It was impulsive. Two and two put together to equal . . . I don't know. I've lived in Cornhill for six years and I've seen what Marilyn Courtney is capable of. I think I know her, what she's all about. The world is full of people like her. Sometimes they end up in jail, sometimes in mental institutions. Some of them become wives or husbands, grandmothers and grandfathers, and they live their lives out more or less peacefully, because—happily for everyone else—things tend to go the way they want them to. Call them amoral, psychopathic, whatever, they're very strong. They know how to make things happen the way they want them to happen, and if somebody's in the way, too bad.

"Marilyn Courtney is one of those people. You aren't. You care about other people. You care a lot—maybe as much as you care about yourself. And I think you know what Marilyn is. You're very intelligent and very sensitive, but you're naïve, too. You think you can help her. You have this idea that you can turn her thinking around. You can't. As much as you might want to, you can't. When she's done with you—when she's done showing off her new, crippled friend—she'll toss you aside. But I think you know that. I think you know everything I've been telling you."

Christine raised an eyebrow, then slowly turned her chair so that her back was to Becky. "Are you done with your coffee?"

"Christine, I——"

"If you're done with your coffee, please leave my house."

"I didn't want to upset you, Christine. I'm sorry."

Christine said nothing. She listened as Becky got out of the wicker chair, heard her move across the room to the wheelchair, felt her hand on her shoulder. "Take care of yourself, Christine."

Moments later she was gone.

Marilyn listened to her pulse in her ears. Jesus, half an hour of pulling and tugging and pushing and she had gotten him only to the base of the attic stairs! How in the hell was she going to get him *up* the stairs? She looked back at the erratic trail of blood that led from Greg's doorway to the side of Brett's head. She'd have to clean that up before Greg saw it, or else he'd start again: "Mommy, why did you hit him? Why did you hit him?" Thankfully, he had shut up almost as soon as she'd told him to. "That's a good boy. Go in the other room until I can get your door fixed, okay? We'll move your bed in later. I've got something to do now."

She opened the attic door, looked up the stairs. She thought the attic would be a good place for him—the useless with the useless, the dead with the dead.

Then she wondered if he *was* dead. From her standing position over him, she saw that his chest was still, and the bleeding near his temple had stopped. Weren't those sure signs of death? She imagined going to her bedroom, getting a mirror, holding it up to his nose. If the mirror stayed clear, he was dead. She decided, at last, that it wasn't necessary. Any fool could see that he was dead: He had that taut and waxy look about him. (An image of her mother laid out primly in the dark mahogany coffin flashed through her mind.) She grimaced, incredulous. Christ, had she really lived with this . . . *thing* for sixteen years? Had she really let it violate her? Now here it lay in its own pee threatening to ruin the smell of her house.

She leaned over, grabbed both of Brett's hands, and started backing up the attic stairs with him. Each time his head flopped backward and hit the edge of a step, she grinned—as if at a small victory.

She hadn't really hit him, Greg told himself. It had been a kind of joke. No, not a joke; a warning—*Stay away from my son!*

She hadn't really hit him. That would be stupid. Nuts. Because they were married. They loved each other; they had to, or they wouldn't be married. And they wouldn't have brought him—Greg—down from heaven to live with them.

But she had looked so angry with that golf club raised high over her head. And happy, too. Angry and happy at the same time. *There, now, you see? That's nuts. Angry and happy at the same time is impossible.*

Greg smiled at the revelation. Everything was better now. He had figured it out. She couldn't have hit him, because it was impossible to be angry and happy at the same time. And that is what he had seen. So, he wasn't seeing things right. He was scared and didn't know what was going on.

He heard a groan beside him on the bed. He froze. The groan was repeated. Greg's breathing stopped.

"My fuckin' balls!" he heard. And then a soft, mature laugh—a laugh he remembered hearing once before, a million years ago. His mind attached a face to that laugh—an angular, intelligent face, and straight blond hair, and lively blue eyes.

"My fuckin' balls are fuckin' killing me!" he heard. His breathing restarted.

He rolled over, onto his left shoulder. The boy's face was silhouetted against the curtainless window.

"Hi," the boy said, though he didn't turn his head to look at Greg. "Long time no see."

Greg could think of nothing to say.

"Cat got your tongue?" said the boy. "Cat got your tongue, cat got your tongue?"

Greg watched, fascinated, frightened, as the silhouette of the boy's lips moved slightly when he talked.

"Or did she take it?"

"Who?"

"*Who?* Her! That goddamned cow that locked you in here, that bitch's bitch, that maniacal mama of yours—*her!*"

"Don't . . . don't . . ." Greg faltered.

"Yes?"

"Don't you say those things about her."

"How old are you?"

"Nine. Older'n you, I bet."

The boy laughed aloud. "Hell, I'm ageless, yeah. Didn't you know that? All us vampires are ageless. Wanna know my name? Ask me my name."

"How'd you get in here?"

"My name's Little Rat. Did I tell you that before? Yeah, it's Little Rat. Good name, huh? Uh-oh, maniacal mama's coming." He got out of the bed, crossed quickly to the window, stepped to the right of it. And was hidden by the darkness.

A moment later the door opened. Marilyn poked her head into the room. She said nothing. She had heard a child crying. But Greg, she could see, was asleep.

He guessed it was morning. Or dusk. It depended, he knew, on the window he was seeing. If it was an east-facing window, then it was morning; a west-facing window, dusk. The light alone was too diffuse, too color-less for him to tell. That fact told him he was in trouble, that his vision had been affected, because the image of the window was not so much an image as a yellowish-white blotch on his eyes and consciousness. And it was growing very slowly, but noticeably, dimmer.

It was dusk.

So, he had a grasp on the time of day.

But not, he realized instantly, on the day itself—on whether it was a Tuesday or a Wednesday—or, to any extent at all, on how long he had been here.

In the attic!

And a grasp on the place she had put him.

She? he wondered. *She?*

Who?

No grasp on who. Or why. Only a feeling of ur-gency, as if someone were calling to him: *Help me!*

And he had an awful need for sleep.

Because there was far more comfort in that than in watching himself die.

"I had a dog once," Greg said. "A puppy."

Little Rat looked interested.

Greg continued: "My dad said he was a dalmatian, 'cause he was white with little black spots." He grinned a small, sad grin. "But I think he was really just a mutt. He had long hair all over his nose, and one green eye and one brown eye." He paused. "His left eye was the green one, I think. Or maybe it was the right one that was green." He stopped. He didn't want to go on, because he knew that Little Rat wanted to know everything about the puppy, and he wasn't sure he could tell him everything without crying. This part was okay; it was the nice part.

"How old was he?" asked Little Rat.

Greg wondered how he'd known that that was what he was going to talk about next. "My dad said he was about eight weeks old. He wasn't a big puppy. My dad said he'd never get *real* big. He said he'd just be average size, but that he was a real smart breed." Another pause. "My dad said he needed a home and that I could give him as good a home as anyone."

Little Rat glanced around the room. "Did he sleep in here, with you?"

"No," Greg answered, his voice low. "He slept in the garage. My mom didn't want him in the house. She said he was dirty. She said he'd pee on everything."

Little Rat waited for Greg to continue.

"My dad made a little house in the garage for him, wrote his name over the door and everything."

"Yeah?" said Little Rat. "What was his name?"

"Charlie. I named him. I thought it fit. He looked like a Charlie, know what I mean? He was real friendly, friendliest pup I ever saw. He woulda been a great dog, my dad said." Greg could feel the tears starting.

Little Rat said, "He died, huh?"

"Yeah." Greg sniffled. "My dad and me were playin' in the yard with him and he ran into the street and a car hit him." He nodded toward the window. "We buried him 'longside the garage. My dad said he'd be warm there 'cause it was away from the wind. I knew he didn't need to be warm no more; I knew he was dead."

"Buried him next to the garage, huh?"

"Yeah. It was a good place. He used to play around there a lot. He used to have this fake bone—leather, ya know—and he used to play with it. Used to try and tear it away from me. He was pretty strong. I buried it with him. I thought . . ." He stopped.

"Yeah?" coaxed Little Rat.

"I thought, ya know, that if he had some little spirit—his ghost—I thought that buryin' him with that fake bone, and where he liked to play, that he could go on playin' there forever."

"I had a cat once," Little Rat said, "and when it died, I buried it with a little toy mouse that it liked to play with, 'cause I thought the same thing."

"My mother dug Charlie up," Greg said. The tears were gone. His voice was suddenly filled with bitterness. "She put him in a garbage can for the garbage men to take away. She said that dead things brought rats around. She said that dead is dead, and the quicker I knew that, the quicker I'd be a man."

Little Rat said nothing.

"I caught her diggin' him up," Greg went on. The bitterness had been replaced by a kind of tight resignation, as if he were asleep and about to have one of his nightmares and knew there was nothing he could do about it. "She showed me his little body on the shovel and she said I should take a long, hard look at it, that it was where we'd all end up someday, so I had to take what I could get."

"What'd she mean by that?" asked Little Rat.

"I don't know," Greg answered.

June 12, 1961

Damn that kid! Damn her! They'd found out because of her. She'd suffered through all those stupid, embarrassing questions because of her. Because of her freakin' big mouth. Damn her to hell!

"What were you thinking about, Miss King? Was it a joke?"

"I told you, I didn't call *anyone!*"

"Miss King, you can forget your denials. We do not believe you."

"I don't care *what* you freakin' believe."

It was clear that the child hated her—crystal clear; otherwise she would have kept her big mouth shut.

"You caused Mrs. Vanderburg no end of heartache. You're quite lucky she's not going to press charges; otherwise you'd find yourself in a juvenile home."

"But I keep telling everyone, I didn't *do* anything."

"Mrs. Williams was more philosophic about the whole matter. She said you were a very troubled girl. And that's why you're here. We have decided that you may need counseling. Do *you* think you need counseling, Miss King?"

So, let the kid cry! Let her! If she was wet, so what? If she was cold, so what? If she was thirsty, or afraid of the dark, or if there were spiders crawling all over her, who gave two shits? The kid deserved *whatever* she got!

"I'm going to ask you some questions you may find uncomfortable."

"I won't answer them."

"It's really in your best interests. We want to help you."

"We? Who's *we?"*

"Everyone who knows you and cares about you. Do you think no one cares about you?"

"I never thought about it."

"Be truthful, now."

"I never thought about it. I *never,* honest to freakin' God, thought about it. Jesus H. Christ, do you think everything I say is a freakin' lie?"

"Of course not. Do you think that's what people think, that you're constantly lying?"

"I never thought about *that,* either. I don't care what people think. I really don't."

Or if she'd caught her hair in the crib springs, or fallen on her oh-so-pretty face, or got zapped into another freakin' dimension, who in the fuck gave a damn?

The baby-sitter examined the rage that was building

inside her; she was fascinated by it. It seemed so powerful, so all-consuming, like a great fire. And she knew she could control it, call it up at will. It was a rage that was almost pleasurable—a kind of sexual pleasure, she supposed.

"Does your, uh . . . your physical development disturb you?"

"Freakin' pervert!"

"That is not my intention in the slightest, young lady, not in the slightest, and you can wipe that grin off your face, too."

"Simpering son-of-a-bitching pervert!"

"Your vocabulary is astounding. Now, will you please answer my question."

"Why?"

"Because we think your answer may have some bearing on what troubles you."

Yes, it was there—her power—easily called up, easily controlled, an easy source of pleasure. Goddamn freakin' little shit-assed kid!

The baby-sitter screamed loud and long. She found pleasure in it—enormous, dizzying pleasure. But there was pain, too, a pain that lingered long after the scream ended—pain in the accusations that had been made, in the questions that had been asked, in the shared, knowing glances.

Damn that kid all to hell!

"We are not communicating, Miss King. I really wish we could communicate."

"Yeah? Is that why you ask about my freakin' tits, you pervert?"

"Young lady, that language is appalling. They are not 'tits'; they are 'breasts.' "

"They sure as fuck are, and they are *big,* aren't they, and you really want to get freakin' hold of 'em, don't ya, huh? Don't ya?"

"You may be excused. And you may return only

when you have decided to use language befitting a young lady."

The baby-sitter despised the pain. The rage and the anger were wonderful, but the pain was nightmarish. And the horror of it was, the rage and the pain were inseparable.

Chapter 28

What happens now? he thought. *I am dying in some-one's cold attic, so what happens now?*

He decided that death was probably a couple days off. He would die of hunger. And of the injury to his head. Or—it was possible—he would die because he didn't know who he was or precisely where he was or why he had been put here. He would die because he was a nonentity.

"Christ!" The word, unintelligible, stumbled off his lips.

He found that he could turn his head slightly. He saw a floor-standing lamp nearby; its cord had been wrapped around its base, and it was minus a shade.

"I don't know, it probably needs rewiring. I'll get to it one of these days."

"Sure you will. Why don't you just put it upstairs, in the attic."

Sure you will . . . He let the voice repeat itself. He winced at the pain; he knew the voice, knew it well. It was a part of him, a part of his life. He was tied to it.

Death was not a pleasant thing to think about. He was used to living, had grown to expect it. He remembered thinking it would be nice to be senile and babbling when death came, and so be ignorant of it.

Dying of a head injury and hunger in someone's cold attic was . . . interesting. And bizarre. If it were someone else it was happening to, and he felt comfortably removed, he would comment sympathetically on it.

"*Look at what it says here. It says this guy was found dead in someone's attic.*"

"*It's no concern of ours, Brett.*"

Brett?

The pain was sudden, and severe, as if the left side of his head had been pumped up with small, pointed stones.

He heard himself scream. He hated himself for it, felt small and helpless.

He smelled anchovies and mint jelly. *Christ! A concussion!*

A wave of nausea flowed over him. It carried the smells with it; it settled on his eyelids and in a thick, undulating line down his stomach.

He turned his head sharply and vomited. He turned his head again, away from the vomit.

He welcomed unconsciousness as if it were an old friend.

It was the first time Marilyn had noticed it and it unsettled her. It was around the eyes, she decided. Something she had seen before, a long time ago. Decades ago. It had unsettled her then, too. She wished she could recall it precisely, pin it down; then, she thought, it wouldn't unsettle her so much.

She went on, wondering how long she had paused: "It's true, Christine: I haven't heard from Brett in days. His secretary and some of his workers have called, wondering where he is and what they're supposed to do, but what can *I* tell them? I haven't the faintest idea where he is." She paused again, looked away.

"Is something wrong, Marilyn?"

Marilyn looked back, saw the concern in Christine's eyes. But, mixed with it, alternating with it, the thing she had seen before—the determination. And the pain. "No, nothing," she said. "I'd tell you if there was."

"I hope you would. I like to think we're friends, Marilyn."

Marilyn looked sharply to the left, toward the stairs. Had Christine heard that scream? She looked back.

"Marilyn, I wish you would tell me what's upsetting you."

Marilyn stared quizzically. How could Christine not have heard? "Nothing." She stopped, listened, expected the scream to be repeated. It wasn't. "I think it's probably just . . . all that's been happening." She stopped again; Greg would have to get a good talking to.

"You must get very lonely here," Christine said.

Marilyn nodded once, grimly. "I do, on occasion. But it's a cross I can bear." She looked again toward the stairs, thought of asking Christine if she'd heard anything, "sort of like a scream." Because there really was no way she could have missed it. "Christine, did you——"

"I'm a cat lover," Christine interrupted. "I always have been. But I hate the sound of a cat fight, don't you?"

Marilyn stared at her, bewildered. "Cat fight?"

"I guess because cats can sound so . . . human."

"Cats?" And, at last, she understood. She smiled a long-suffering smile. "Yes, of course. Personally, I hate cats. Dogs, too. Greg had a puppy once. I believe he thought more of it than he did of me."

Christine smiled. "I'm sure it was your imagination."

"I don't think so, but, at any rate, we were able to get rid of it." She stood. "Could you excuse me just a moment, Christine?"

"Certainly."

"I've got to check on Greg."

"Oh? How is he?"

"His cold is still hanging on, I'm afraid."

"That's a shame. It's been a few days, hasn't it?"

"Almost a week. I'll call the doctor if there's no real improvement soon."

Greg wasn't certain what he'd heard: It had invaded his sleep, transformed his dreams, and awakened him.

He sat up in the huge bed, caught a glimpse of himself in the floor-standing mirror opposite the bed, and looked away quickly.

He wondered if it was Little Rat he'd heard, if Little Rat wanted him to wake up and so had called to him. No, he decided: Little Rat came to this room at night, when it was easier to sneak around. Besides, what he had heard sounded more like a siren. Or a scream. A scream like that he'd heard once before—the night his father left the house.

He climbed determinedly out of the bed. He went to the door. And jumped back, but too late. The door swung open, and hit him hard. He tumbled backward, rolled reflexively. He lay still, on his stomach, momentarily breathless.

Marilyn stepped into the room. "Stand up," he heard.

He hesitated very briefly, then pushed himself to a sitting position. He put his hand on his forehead, took it away, saw a tiny smear of blood on his fingers. "I'm bleeding," he said, and realized that, in jumping back, he had stooped over just enough that the glass doorknob hit him. "I'm bleeding," he repeated, fascinated, disgusted, frightened by the sight of his own blood.

"Stand up," he heard again.

Clumsily, he stood and faced his mother.

"We've discussed this before, haven't we, Greg?"

"Yes, Mommy." He had no idea what she was talking about; he knew only what she wanted him to say.

"And if I remember correctly, the last time we discussed it, Mrs. Bennet was here, too."

The scream! "Yes, Mommy."

"You have almost frightened her to death this time. You realize that, don't you?"

"Yes. I'm sorry."

"Right now she's down in the parlor trying to catch her breath. I think she'll be okay, no thanks to you." She paused, conjured up a look of authority mixed liberally with pity. "You know what this means, don't you?"

He nodded.

"Don't you?"

"Yes."

"I just want you to know that the more you act up, the longer you behave like a little animal, the longer you'll stay here."

He touched his forehead again, looked at his fingers. The bleeding had stopped.

Marilyn stepped toward him; he flinched.

"Yes, Mommy."

Marilyn grinned. "That's a good boy." She moved closer, held her arms out. "Hug me," she cooed.

He stepped forward without hesitation, found himself enveloped in her arms, squeezed to her big, hard breasts. He cringed at the smell of lilac perfume mixed with her nervous perspiration.

"I love you, my Greg," he heard.

The absence of pain confused him. He felt only a small itching sensation at his groin, inside, just above his testicles. And he was lightheaded. He knew that if he stood, he would fall. It was, he realized, the hunger working on him.

"Hello," he whispered. "My name is Brett Courtney," and felt a broad smile spread across his face. He saw himself smiling in his mind's eye and recognized the face. Names and dates and places that were a part of his life nudged at him, shouted at him, flooded back into his consciousness. He closed his eyes tightly, suddenly dizzy and nauseous: The return of identity had overwhelmed him, because with it had come the damn-

ing and awful knowledge that this was *his* attic he was
dying in, and it was *his wife* who had put him here.

He saw that it was night. A dull, creamy light, from
the city itself, had invaded the attic, though not its
farthest corners. And though it was cold here, that light
had a comforting, dreamlike quality. *At this moment
you are safe,* it told him. Because Marilyn was frightened of the attic even in daylight, he could not imagine
that at night she did more than hurry past its door—
especially now that her husband's body lay beyond it.
If in fact she was convinced that he was dead. And
that was something he could not know.

At any rate, there would come a time—perhaps
soon, perhaps the following day—that she would want
to rid her house of him. And if she found him still
alive . . .

Chapter 29

It had been over a week and there were distasteful realities to face. Marilyn had known it would come to this. Time was not about to stop for her. And time brought decay with it, and decay brought——

She thought, suddenly, that she had done few foolish things in her life. She had rarely had to answer to anyone, except once as a teenager and once to Brett, a couple years after Greg was born.

("Listen, Brett, you want another kid, you conceive it. *I* do not want to become pregnant again. I've discovered what pain is, and it doesn't appeal to me."

"But, Marilyn, we've discussed this.")

Asshole! Wanting to populate the world with little carbon copies of himself.

She thought she could smell him already. Rationally, she knew she probably couldn't, because the attic was cold and dry, and decay didn't happen very quickly in cold, dry places.

She plunged her hands deep into the pockets of her housedress, made tight fists, let her hands relax, flexed her fingers.

She had been standing near the front windows. It was midmorning, and a sparse snowfall had started. It wouldn't last long, she knew. In an hour or so the sun would come out, and the couple feet of snow on the ground would begin to melt. Spring was close, she thought; it was going to come early this year.

The phone rang. She jumped at the sound, crossed the large room quickly. It rang again. "Christ!" She snatched up the receiver:

"Yes?"

"Mrs. Courtney?"

"Yes. Who's calling?"

"This is Shirley Wise at the Middle School. I'm calling about your son, Greg."

"Yes?"

"I'd like to know when we can look forward to seeing him again."

Marilyn sensed the woman's forced good humor and was annoyed by it. "That's hard to say, Mrs. Wise."

"*Ms.* Wise."

"*Ms.* Wise. It really is hard to say, because this sickness of his is not at all predictable and——"

"Is he under a doctor's care, Mrs. Courtney?"

"Of course he's under a doctor's care!"

"I was only inquiring, Mrs. Courtney. His classmates do miss him, and we all wish him well."

"Is that all, Ms. Wise?"

"Yes, thank you. Oh, by the way, we'll be sending some work home to him, if you don't mind, if you think he's up to it."

"I'd rather you didn't do that, Ms. Wise. I'd rather he was allowed to rest."

"Oh, yes, of course. Please keep us informed, Mrs. Courtney."

"I'll do that, Ms. Wise."

Marilyn hung up. She tapped her foot against the rug, folded her arms over her breasts. She frowned. *Problems,* she thought. *Always problems.*

The itch was on the inside of her left wrist. A nervous itch; if she ignored it, it would go away. She scratched the wrist, at first lightly. The itch persisted. "Damn!" She scratched harder, became aware that she could feel the itch beneath her nails, as if it were inside, on the bone, taunting her. "Damn it to hell!" She went through the skin; a tiny bead of blood appeared.

The itch vanished. She smiled, relieved, and watched the bead grow, become a drop. She held the wrist up so that the blood could run. "Good," she said, and sucked delicately at it.

The flow of blood soon stopped.

She pulled the attic door open.

The stench moved over her like syrup. Her breathing stopped in reaction to it. She slammed the door shut, leaned with her back against it, her arms wide, as if to hold it closed, as if the stench were a physical thing.

The itch settled in her right wrist. She threw herself away from the door and down the hallway to her bedroom.

She sat trembling on the edge of the bed, her nails working hard at her wrist, trying in vain to destroy the itch there.

She opened the armoire door slowly, carefully. There were treasures here, a life here. She lifted out one photograph, then another, and set them in the box beside her on the floor. Again she reached into the armoire, picked out some more photographs—a dozen of them—put them in the box. Eventually, the box was filled. She put her hands on the flaps to close it and saw Brett's face looking up at her, here and there wearing a photographic smile, all his teeth straight and white. She grinned back at him and closed the box. *The past is the past,* she thought. *Why leave its props lying around cluttering things up?*

She carried the box to the back door, opened it, crossed to the garage, went around the side of it to the back, where the garbage cans were. She searched until she found an empty one, then dumped the photographs in. She smiled hugely. The sound of metal hitting metal and glass breaking pleased her. She wished it could continue for longer than just a few moments.

Greg said, "She's throwing something away." He turned from the window. "She's throwing something away," he repeated.

"Yeah," said Little Rat. He was seated on the floor, his back against the bed's long side, his hands behind his head, his legs outstretched. "I know she is."

Greg turned back to the window. "She's coming back now. I wonder what she threw away."

"I *know* what she threw away," Little Rat said, and he grinned a big, wide, gloating grin. "But I ain't gonna tell ya."

"Why aren't ya?"

" 'Cause ya wouldn't know what I was talking about, that's why."

"Sure I would."

Little Rat seemed to think about that a moment. Then: "Okay, what if I told ya it was the past she threw away? What would ya say about that?"

Greg didn't know what to say about it. As far as he was concerned, it was dumb, because it was impossible to throw the past away. The past wasn't real, and only real things got thrown into trash cans.

Greg laughed. Little Rat had told him a joke, and though he didn't get it, he wasn't about to let Little Rat know.

Little Rat was suddenly standing; Greg's false laughter died instantly. Sometimes Little Rat scared him.

"I'm sorry," Greg said.

Little Rat glared at him. Greg hated it when Little Rat glared; he looked so angry, so round-eyed, so . . . hollow. Like a marionette.

The look softened. "I got to be going," he said. He turned and started for the door.

"When you comin' back?" Greg called.

Little Rat made no reply. He put his hand on the

doorknob, turned it, opened the door, and left the room. The door slammed shut after him.

Greg's mouth dropped open. He ran to the door. He tried the knob. The door was locked.

Brett was certain of everything now except the one thing that could save him—a way out. And mobility. He cursed himself for not knowing the layout of the attic better than he did. After fifteen years in this house, he thought he knew every room, every corner. But the house was still strange to him. He knew only those rooms he used daily. And he had used the attic only a few times, to store old furniture and boxes of miscellaneous things. He thought of *himself,* suddenly, as a miscellaneous thing, a thing that had outlived its usefulness. It was the way Marilyn thought of him, he realized.

Christ, how had this happened to him? How, after sixteen years, could he have failed to see her for what she was? And did he *know* what she was, or was he only guessing? The word *psychopathic* was very convenient, but it meant nothing, really. It was a label, and it solved none of his problems; it only magnified them.

His most important task, he knew, was to attempt movement, because if he was unable to move, he was dead: Either she would end it for him, or he would die, slowly, agonizingly, of thirst or hunger. And if he could move, then he had to find a way out. Down the main stairway would probably be suicide, and he couldn't go out the window, of course.

"Stack those boxes up over there, Brett. We'll never use that stairwell, anyway."

Brett replayed the words mentally. What boxes? he wondered. What stairwell? Were there *two* attic exits?

He felt a migraine starting. *No, goddamnit, not now!* He saw the migraine as a kind of ragtag, malevolent hobo come to pick at his brains and take away whatever sense was left in them. He watched the hobo lean over him, watched the hobo reach for him, grinning as if satisfied. He turned his head violently away from those hands. And saw the boxes that Marilyn had been talking about years ago. And knew where the stairwell was. He tried reaching for it, like a drowning man for a thrown oar. But his arms lay heavy and stiff and immobile at his sides. Only his fingers moved slightly.

And the grinning hobo was upon him.

Chapter 30

The whole dream was coming apart. Christine didn't know why it should: It was only a small dream, and, at the beginning, not even hers but Tim's. *A home of our own.* She remembered thinking—how long ago?—that it was a foolish dream and hoping Tim would forget it. And she remembered seeing this little house for the first time, remembered wanting it as she had never before wanted anything.

A very small dream—small and mundane, like wanting a new dryer. *A home of our own.* It no longer meant anything. It was lost in that other thing, that other—— Christ, what was it? A thing like anger, or rage, and so tenacious, tenacious as a leech. A part of her, yes—she knew it was part of her, like a cancer would be part of her.

She didn't want to believe she could be dying. She fought the belief. She told herself she was tired from overwork, tired from the adjustment to her new life-style, tired from trying to be all that Tim wanted her to be. But these were lies. She knew they were lies. Her last piece of work was the painting done during the winter's worst blizzard, two months ago. That painting scared her now. She had shut it up in a closet. And Cornhill, and the house, demanded no burdensome adjustment. The people here were neither overly friendly nor overly aloof; they were very much like the people she and Tim had left behind when they moved here.

206

And Tim expected nothing from her that she was unable to give. He never had.

So, her excuses meant nothing, and the awful fact remained: She could look into her future and see nothing. A blank. Only this day, and the next, and the next, and perhaps a dozen, two dozen more. Then nothing. Because something inside her—a part of her—was slowly, and certainly, killing her.

The ringing of the phone jarred her. She looked over at it, startled, suddenly weakened. She took a deep breath, then another, wheeled herself to it, lifted the receiver:

"Hello?" It was a whisper; her strength had not yet returned.

"Christine, did I disturb you?"

"No, Marilyn. I'm a little out of breath. It's all right."

"I can call back later."

"No. I'm okay now." She hesitated, felt her strength coming back. "Honest, I'm okay."

"Good," Marilyn said, and paused dramatically. "Can you come over? I have a little surprise for you. You like surprises, don't you?"

"Surprise? Sure. Just give me a few minutes."

"Great. I'll see you soon, then." She hung up.

Marilyn beamed with pride at the top of the short, newly installed ramp. Christine, at the bottom of the ramp, shook her head slowly, her lips tight, in mock disapproval.

"Marilyn, I asked you not to do this. It wasn't necessary." And then she grinned. "You really shouldn't have, Marilyn. But now that you have . . ." Her grin became a big, sincere smile. "Now that you have, thank you. Very much."

Marilyn gestured impatiently at the low metal railings on either side of the ramp. "Aren't you going to try it?"

"Sure I am." Christine grabbed the railings and pulled herself quickly, expertly, up to the landing, where Marilyn waited. "It works the way it's supposed to, Marilyn."

Marilyn put her hand on the doorknob. "I even had this door rehung, Christine." She opened the door. It had opened outward from left to right; now it opened from right to left, away from Christine.

"Perfect," Christine said, pleased all over again. "Everything's absolutely perfect." She touched Marilyn's hand. "Thank you, Marilyn. It's the nicest surprise I've had in a long, long time."

"My pleasure, Christine." She nodded toward the inside of the house. "Shall we? It's awfully cold out here."

"Yes," Christine said.

Greg wondered about several things. He wondered if his mother really would put a TV in here, like she said she was going to. And he wondered when he would go back to school and see Jimmy and Leon and Mark again. And Coni. They were all his friends, and they were probably wondering what had happened to him.

And he wondered when he had last eaten. He thought it had been two days ago. Meat loaf and peas and some milk. Or maybe hot dogs and milk. He wasn't sure. He remembered Little Rat—who had come in just after he'd started eating—saying that it looked like slop and that he should have thrown it in his mother's face. Greg hadn't liked that remark: "She's my mother," he remembered saying, and Little Rat had laughed and said, "So what?" To which Greg had said nothing.

And he wondered if he should block up the bottom of the closet door to help contain the smell of his bowel movements. The shoe box he'd found had probably fallen apart by now. The smell came to him in waves—a sickly sweet smell, the strident odor of decay.

For now he merely sat quietly, his back against the edge of the bed, his legs outstretched, and his hands behind his head. Sitting this way really wasn't as comfortable as Little Rat had made it look; it hurt his tailbone, and his knuckles where he had his fingers intertwined.

And he wondered when his mother would tell him why, exactly, she had shut him up in this room.

He was sure she would tell him sooner or later.

She was his mother, after all.

"I consider you my closest friend, Christine."

Marilyn had brought a small, straight-backed wooden chair in from the dining room and placed it in front of Christine. Both chairs were parallel to the front windows. The drapes were open, and Christine noticed that a heavy rain had started—patches of brownish-green grass were visible on Marilyn's front lawn.

"I haven't had many close friends," Marilyn continued. "None as close as you. Even in high school I was pretty much—what's the word?—a loner. By choice, of course. The few friendships I did have just" —she waved at the air with her right hand—"vanished. Poof! Like that. People found it hard to understand me. I suppose—yes, I'll admit it—I expected too much from them. I expected things like loyalty and respect, and I guess that was too much to expect. But you're different, Christine. I sensed it from the moment we met. You value friendships as highly as I do, and you probably expect as much from one as I. Am I right or wrong?"

Christine said nothing. She nodded once, slowly, solemnly.

"I thought so," Marilyn continued. "I thought so. I knew it when you broke off with that Foster woman. *I* knew she was no good—well, she *is* a lesbian, isn't she—because I've known her for a few years. But you're new here, and though I warned you, I couldn't really expect you to trust the word of a woman who was little more than a stranger. So I let you find out for yourself. I knew how perceptive and discerning you were. I knew."

"Thank you, Marilyn." Christine's tone was low, confidential.

"Friends don't say 'Thank you.' Friends expect . . . what they receive: trust and respect and loyalty. I had that ramp built because you are my friend, my closest friend, and you have certain very special needs. I would not be your friend if I didn't understand that."

"Not many people do understand it, Marilyn."

"I believe you. I know what people are and what they're capable of. I've seen it a thousand times. I'm sure you have, too."

Christine nodded again, again solemnly.

"We're kindred spirits, Christine. We see things the same way. We're very much like sisters. I believe we even think the same way."

"Perhaps we do, Marilyn."

"Would you like some tea, Christine?"

"Yes, I would. I'd love some tea."

The cat, an orange-and-white longhair with a small round face, huge round eyes, and small ears—her erstwhile owners were fond of calling her a Persian—had given the young German shepherd two impossibly quick swipes, each tracing thin, painful scratches along the dog's nose. The shepherd had supposed the cat's great bulk would prevent her from running and make her easy prey—much like the kitten he had savaged the week before. But, at last, his overconfidence had made him dangerously incautious, and he had learned what a cornered fully grown cat could do.

The cat had no time to gloat over her victory; she

had more important business. The time had come for her kittens to be born, and she was a long way from the safe, warm place she had selected only days before.

The pain struck her; she panted to relieve it, and soon it dissipated.

She was a very resourceful cat. She had learned quickly to live on what she could forage, or kill. And she—like all cats—was an expert killer. Her memories of her last owners were vague, meaningless ("The goddamned cat is pregnant again." . . . "Jesus Christ, how long is this going to go on?" . . . "Get rid of her if you don't like it." . . . "That's precisely what I intend to do.").

She ran. The dog would return soon, and it was likely he'd bring other dogs with him. And the warm, safe place she had chosen seemed very appealing now, the call to motherhood loud and powerful within her.

She recognized the house immediately, both because of its scent and its great size. She went around to the back of the house, stopped, panted a moment. And leaped five feet up the trunk of the huge maple. She climbed furiously until the top of the tree was only a few feet above her.

She looked. The open window was close; she could almost step to it.

The pain struck her once more. She panted briefly, then leaped again—through the window, to the attic floor.

And felt something tear inside her belly. The pain was overwhelming now; she purred loudly, coarsely, in reaction to it.

She moved to the open space she had found in the attic floorboards, near the stairs, and crawled in.

An hour later, six kittens were nursing from her.

Eight hours later, she left the attic through the open window in search of food for herself. She felt sure her kittens were in no danger; the place she had chosen under the attic floor was dark and safe and warm.

After a short search, she killed a mouse. Her intention now was to bring it back to the attic and eat it there, while her kittens—their hunger nearly insatiable—continued nursing from her.

It was a greater effort this time to scale the huge maple. She was still tired from giving birth, and the mouse between her teeth was a clumsy burden. She found it necessary to rest several times.

The mistress of the house closed and locked the attic window during the third of the cat's short rests. She had felt a marked draft in the house, had called her husband, had been told the probable source of the draft.

The woman left the attic quickly. Not until a month and a half later would she enter it again. And then another time, a week after that.

Attics frightened her. But they were good for hiding things.

Strength came to him and went from him in waves, as if in time with an incredibly slow heartbeat. And the fact that he was blind here, in this stairwell, and had no idea where it led, made him feel smothered—a participant in someone else's nightmare.

He had heard Marilyn open and close the main attic door. And he had waited resignedly for her footfalls on the stairs. But there hadn't been any. Only a return to silence. That was when he had allowed himself a rest.

Mobility had come to him slowly, and moving the boxes that blocked the stairwell required a strength he assumed had left him days ago.

Now, halfway down, resting was involuntary.

He had no idea what he'd do if he found a way out. No idea at all. Marilyn, he realized, needed help. Or punishment. That concept intrigued him, and for several moments he involved himself with several delicious fantasies. It amazed him that he was not above punishing her in some way. In his own way. But that was for later.

And there was Greg to consider—Greg, his only offspring; Marilyn's prisoner. Christ, that was obscene!

But now his own safety, his own life, concerned him most.

Because, he realized, unless he used more strength and tenacity than he had, he would probably die here.

Marilyn hit her thumb with the hammer. And cursed aloud. How in the hell was she supposed to drive these little tacks into the wood? The damned hammer was almost useless. She stuck her thumb into her mouth and grimaced at the smell that wafted up to her from under the door. She'd have to cover the entire perimeter of the door, seal the attic off entirely. She wondered if she had enough plastic for that. She wondered if, in time, the stench would penetrate the walls and floors to the rooms below, and fill the whole house with that abominable stink. She furiously nailed another section of plastic to the bottom of the door. No way in hell was he going to continue to corrupt *her* house.

Chapter 31

"Hey, Greg, you in there?"

Greg felt the blanket being tugged. It had become his habit to sleep with the blanket covering his entire body, from the bottoms of his feet to the top of his head. It was safer that way. The things that crawled around on the floor and that fell from the ceiling at night were stopped by a good heavy blanket. And it was warmer, too. Especially here, in this room. He wondered if his mother would really have the radiator fixed, like she said. He decided she probably would. She *said* she would.

"Greg, come on outa there. What you scared of?"

It was a good question, Greg thought. And the answer was simple: He was scared of Little Rat. Scared of the way he glared, like a marionette. Scared of the things he said about his—Greg's—mother, things that made Greg angry. Scared of the way he could open doors that Greg couldn't. Scared of the way he could appear here at any old time he wanted. And scared because it was probably true what he had said a long time ago: He was a vampire.

"Hey, Greg, you're fulla shit, you know that?" Little Rat chuckled a low, taunting chuckle. "You really are."

"No I'm not," Greg whispered.

"Sure you are. Your whole family is, 'specially your mother."

Greg said nothing. He had an idea what was com-

214

ing. Maybe if he kept quiet, Little Rat would go away. He decided, suddenly, that he hated Little Rat.

"Remember that story you told me about the puppy —the one your mother dug up?"

Greg stayed quiet.

"Yeah," Little Rat went on, "well, that was a shitty story. That was a real shitty story. It probably wasn't even true. I'll bet three spits it wasn't true."

"It was true," Greg whispered. He felt the blanket being tugged harder.

"Come on *outa* there, Greg. I can't hear what you're sayin'."

Greg felt the blanket yanked away. He rolled in the bed toward Little Rat, eyes wide.

And gasped. The word "Mommy!" escaped him, and he buried his head in the pillow to shut himself away from what stood beside the bed.

"She's a damned freakin' old bitch!" it yelled. And Greg imagined the words moving out of the motionless, dark oval mouth, and the dark eyes in the pasty-white face grinning madly at him.

Little Rat had changed.

"Mommy!" Greg whimpered.

"A freakin' greedy old witch, yeah, and she's gonna let ya starve here, to death——"

"Mommy!" Greg screamed.

"In your own shit——"

The door burst open. The overhead light came on. Marilyn screeched, "Shut up you goddamned little bastard I'm trying to sleep can't you see that?" And Greg was amazed, petrified, that she had said it all in one breath.

"Mommy?" he whispered.

The overhead light went out. The door slammed shut. Seconds later another door, down the hall, slammed shut.

Little Rat said, "Neat trick, huh? I can do it for ya again. Wanna see?"

Greg had curled up into a fetal position. He said nothing. He wanted desperately to get away from this thing that was sharing his room with him.

"Christine, wake up." Tim nudged her. "Darling?" He flicked on the bedside lamp. "My God!" Her face, neck, and shoulders were bathed in perspiration, and her body shook convulsively. He put his hand to her cheek; the skin was incredibly hot.

Tim scrambled out of bed, ran to the living room, snatched up the phone. He hesitated. It would be best, he reasoned, to call an ambulance. He couldn't be certain Christine's doctor was available now and might waste precious time finding out. He got the phone book, opened it.

"Tim?"

He looked toward the bedroom. "Christine?"

He dropped the phone book and hurried into the bedroom. She was sitting up, her head thrown back against the headboard, her arms limp at her sides. She looked exhausted.

"I was just about to call an ambulance," he said. "I thought you were sick."

"I was." She smiled weakly. "I guess I still am."

"I'll call the doctor." He started to leave the room.

"No, Tim." He stopped. "It's not necessary." She paused. "It was only a nightmare."

Tim looked incredulously at her. "It must have been one hell of a nightmare. You should have seen yourself."

"Yes, Tim, it *was* one hell of a nightmare."

"Do you want to talk about it?"

She shook her head. "No, I don't. I can't."

Tim went over to her, sat on the edge of the bed. "It might be better for you if you talked about it, Christine. It's obvious you're sublimating something——"

"I can't talk about it, Tim, because I don't remember it."

"You don't remember it? How can you not remember it? I don't understand."

"All I remember is that Jimmy Wheeler was in it."

"Jimmy Wheeler? Who's Jimmy Wheeler?"

Christine sighed. "That little boy, the one I met in the park. You remember—I did his portrait."

Tim remembered. "Oh, you mean the boy who died."

Christine looked pained. "Yes."

"I'm sorry." He took her hand, caressed it. "I didn't mean to sound insensitive. I just didn't know he meant that much to you."

"Apparently he does, Tim."

"Yes," Tim murmured, "I can see that." He paused, then: "I can still call Dr. Tichell, Christine."

"Not now, Tim."

He stood, went over to his side of the bed. "If it happens again, Christine, I'm calling the doctor."

"I hope you do, Tim. And if you do, I hope he can help."

A half-hour later, the thought that accompanied Christine into sleep was: *I am dying. Something inside, a part of me, is slowly killing me. And there's nothing I can do about it.*

Chapter 32

It didn't make any sense to Greg, but it didn't need to. She had good reasons for shutting him up in here and not feeding him very much (which was okay, he thought, because he didn't feel hungry anymore, just thirsty) and keeping the radiator broken. It was cold, sure, but at least he had this heavy blanket. He wished he had a TV, though. There were no hours here, just mornings and afternoons and evenings. A TV would let him count the hours, and the half-hours, and, something inside him said, that would make the wait here a little easier.

She would tell him what her reasons were soon enough. Because she loved him. She had said it more than once. She had said it a million times: "I love you, my Greg." A zillion times.

He wondered, suddenly, what she meant.

He heard the door being unlocked. He looked toward it. The door opened.

Marilyn, a tray of food in hand, stepped into the room. She didn't bother to turn on the light; it was nearly dawn.

"Greg"—she kicked the door closed—"I'm sorry. Can you forgive me? I was sitting and talking with Mrs. Bennet about one thing and another, and we got onto the subject of food—she was giving me a recipe, I believe—and I suddenly remembered I hadn't fed you in a long, long time." She grinned hugely. "So I

218

hurried to the market and I bought all the things you like so much." She held the tray out so he could see what was on it. "Macaroni and cheese," she said, "peanut-butter-and-jelly sandwiches—grape jelly—lemonade, and some root beer, too, and over here"—she pointed happily—"spinach (it always amazed me, my Gregory, that you liked spinach so much), and some salad with Russian dressing, and, for dessert, sherbet and whipped cream (I must confess, Gregory, that I like that, too) and pound cake." She rushed to the bed with the tray of food, held it out to him. He pushed himself to a sitting position and took the tray. He was bewildered, a little frightened, speechless. "And then, my Greg, when you're done with that, you can settle down and watch TV." She gestured toward the door.

And vanished.

Greg stifled a gasp.

The tray of food vanished.

And Greg felt suddenly hollow, alone, like a bamboo fishing pole tossed overboard and allowed to drift.

She's going to let me starve to death!

No she won't.

She couldn't.

She was his mother!

He still felt the metal tray in his hands, still smelled the cheese, and the jelly. And, strangely, the smells made him a little sick—the way taco smell made him sick. He needed to vomit, suddenly, but knew if he did it would hurt, because there was nothing in his stomach. He fought the smells back, and very slowly his nausea disappeared.

He grinned at the small victory.

And felt Little Rat lie down beside him.

"A freakin' goddamned old scumbag, yeah——"

"Don't," Greg hissed, his clenched fists suddenly pressed hard to his ears. "Don't!"

"She crawled out from under some kinda slimy rock

and she was draggin' you behind her." He chuckled that low, earthy chuckle. "Yeah, you were fallin' outa her, *fallin' outa her* she was so slimy——"

Greg had never imagined he could move so fast. One moment his right fist was at his ear—though it did no good; he still heard Little Rat—and the next it was connecting with something hard, but something that gave, too, under pressure, something that snapped dully, like a live, moist twig.

He heard a quick, short-lived gurgling noise, then realized that Little Rat's weight was off the bed. Greg rolled over and opened his eyes wide. "Mommy!" he screeched, so loud it hurt his ears and throat and made bile creep into his mouth.

Little Rat was tearing madly at his own throat, as if there were something awful inside it and the only way to get it out was through the skin and bone. And he was stumbling around the room, like his legs were slowly breaking. And hoarse "ak-ak" noises were coming from him. And every other second he turned his head and stared round-eyed, accusingly, at Greg.

"Mommy! Mommy!"

Little Rat crumpled near the window, lay still on his back, hands still at his throat.

Greg screamed again, and again, and again. Until the bedroom door burst open. Until Marilyn crossed the room, her hand raised, and he saw that horrible smile on her face. Until he saw that she had left the door open. Until he jumped from the bed, ran across the room, through the open door, down the hall-way——

He stopped screaming, at last, when he felt the cold air of the early spring morning through his pajamas.

He wondered where he was. Behind the garage, he realized.

And his mother was in front of it, calling to him: "My Gregory? My Gregory?"

He knew what she would do with him: She would shut him up in that room again. With Little Rat.

"Gregory, you're going to catch your death."

He could hear her coming around to the side of the garage now. He glanced about. He knew Cornhill well; he had lived in the district all his life. He knew that it was big, but not awfully big, and that downtown was about a thirty-minute walk from here. Or a fifteen-minute run.

"Please, Gregory, Mommy needs you——"

He ran. Through a dozen back yards and a dozen front yards, over a half-dozen fences, causing a dozen chained dogs to bark wildly. He ran wildly, certain she was behind him, right behind him, her outstretched hand almost on him, and Little Rat—his hands still at his throat, those "ak-ak" noises still coming from him—right behind her.

He ran until he collapsed, barely able to breathe. He looked up. The morning sun cast the raised letters above the doorway in harsh relief: "Sibley Building." It was the right place.

He closed his eyes.

It was like watching some pretentious avant-garde movie, Marilyn thought. Still, there was much to be said for it, real benefit to be gained from it.

She had never before been able to weep spontaneously. She remembered weeping only once, as a girl, and then out of need, because tears had been expected from her, because, if she failed to produce tears, eyebrows would be raised and accusations made.

But now . . .

Six hours . . . She thought it was pathetic, and wonderful, that she had actually wept without stopping for six hours. And much of it—all of it?—was genuine. But it had been progressive—at first a heavy, heart-thumping, throat-closing remorse. Greg had run from her, he was afraid of her, he *hated* her, at last. It was a phrase that stayed with her, that lingered in the darkest corners of her remorse for the first two, three hours—during the time her remorse was for her loss, the loss of her son. A time when her senses dulled, and her vision blurred, and she felt certain her whole beautiful, ordered world was coming apart. Then, gradually, the truth of the phrase revealed itself to her:

At last! At last! Greg hated her. At last!

And, in that moment, the cause for her weeping changed. The weeping itself changed; occasional squeals of almost childish laughter came into it.

Greg hated her at last!

It had been so terribly obvious, she hadn't even seen it:

Only one thing really mattered. Not Brett, that whoremongering, abhorrent bastard stinking her house up; no, not him! And not Greg, always sniveling at her, calling her "Mommy" as though she were some ghastly, milk-producing, soft-skinned moron who would one day be a grandmother and *that's* what she did with *her* life; no, not Greg!

Only the house, big and eternal; only the house mattered.

Greg and Brett had been trespassers in it. They had corrupted it, dirtied it, trespassed in it. Just as they had trespassed on her. Through her. And into her.

Greg hated her at last!

Her scheme to rid herself of him, and to rid her house of him, had worked at last. *At last!*

She looked at the clock: 12:15. It was time.

She got out of her wing chair, crossed to the telephone, lifted it, got the phone book from beneath it. She turned to the yellow pages, looked under "Antiques—Dealers." She knew the value of what she was selling. She'd make a pretty penny. She wouldn't tell anyone it had all been dirtied, soiled, corrupted. She cringed. Christ, could she imagine, could she imagine? —the whole house, even the walls. But not the attic. It was sealed now.

She would call the painters later.

Part Three

THE HOUSE

Chapter 33

June 19, 1961

Alone! I am all alone! And nobody will help me! The child's thoughts were not as clear as that, but, in substance, said as much. She tried to move, and couldn't. Tried to cry out, but her fear stopped her.

She waited. There was no pain. Only numbness. And confusion.

After many minutes, the baby-sitter turned the TV down; it was ruining her concentration. She glanced at the telephone on the small white table just inside the entrance to the kitchen.

Later, she thought.

One thing was certain: Six months of dull Friday nights shouldn't have ended like this. There was no reason for it to have come to this. Well, her own stupidity was the reason, wasn't it? Her own colossal stupidity. . . .

She stood, went to the telephone, picked up the receiver dialed, waited.

"Hello?" she heard.

"Is Mrs. Winter there, please?" she said.

"May I ask who's calling?"

"Her baby-sitter. This is her baby-sitter."

"Just a moment."

She heard, as if from a distance, "Evelyn, it's for you. Your baby-sitter."

She waited again. Then: "Yes, this is Mrs. Winter."

"Mrs. Winter?"

"What is it? Is something wrong?"

"I don't know, Mrs. Winter." The baby-sitter paused briefly. "I mean . . . it's the baby——"

"The baby? What's happened to the baby?"

"Nothing. I mean . . . I don't know. She's so quiet. I think you'd better come home, Mrs. Winter."

"Quiet? What do you mean *quiet?*"

"Well, I mean she's breathing and everything, but . . . she's not moving. She fell. Out of her crib. She fell."

A short silence.

"Mrs. Winter?"

Then, again as if from a distance: "Oh, Jesus!" And a click, a dial tone.

The baby-sitter put the receiver on its rest. She went back to the child's room, turned the light on.

She saw that the child was almost exactly as she had left her—on her side at the back of the crib—except now her huge, impossibly blue eyes were open.

Would she tell? wondered the baby-sitter. Would the child tell her parents what had happened? Would she say something like, "I pee-peed, and I got her wet, and she said a bad thing and threw me down, real hard"? Would she say something like that? Or would it all end right here? Because the child was too damned scared and confused. Yes, she decided. It would all end right here.

She saw that the child was staring at her. Hard. Not with a bubbling smile ready on her lips, as if the baby-sitter were merely an object of amusement or curiosity. But hard. And cold. In emotion so intense that the muscles of the child's face had frozen, and all the energy in her small, quiet body had massed in the eyes.

Chapter 34

It had been a long morning for Roger Peterson, and it promised to be an even longer afternoon. There were exactly twenty-three Courtneys in the Rochester section of the phone book and, he estimated, at least a dozen more for the outlying towns. But that was all the police had been able to give him—the boy's last name, Courtney, and a description: eight or nine years old, four feet six inches tall, eighty-five pounds, sandy-blond hair, large gray eyes. A good-looking boy. And Roger Peterson had some bad news: The boy was in Intensive Care at Highland Hospital. The boy had been able to tell police only his name—his whole name, though the first part had been unintelligible—before slipping into unconsciousness. Now the boy was coma-tose. The temperature had just risen to twenty degrees when they found him—dressed only in light-blue cotton pajamas—curled up in front of the Sibley Building. No one knew precisely how long he'd been there. "A couple hours at least," was the attending physician's guess. "I'm really surprised nobody noticed him."

Roger Peterson called the tenth Courtney of the afternoon.

"Hello?"

A woman's voice—a young woman, Peterson thought. "Is this the Courtney residence?"

"Yes, it is, and we've got all the life insurance and all the magazines——"

"This is Roger Peterson, ma'am, from the Department of Social Services."

"Oh? Are you peddling food stamps over the phone now?"

"Mrs. Courtney, please, I'm calling in reference to——"

"Or are you passing out those welfare checks to just anyone? We happen to be white, Mr. Peterson."

"Do you have a son, Mrs. Courtney?"

"A son? No, I don't have a son."

"Thank you, Mrs. Courtney." He hung up. "For Christ's sake," he whispered.

Obviously the boy had been abandoned, hard to believe as that was; otherwise there would have been panicked calls to every official agency in the city by now. It had been over twelve hours since the boy was found.

Peterson checked his log sheet. Of the ten Courtneys called, three apparently were not home, two—a Mark Courtney and a B. Courtney—yielded busy signals, two were elderly people, one number was "no longer assigned," and two were obvious blind alleys.

He dialed the eleventh number. Surely something would happen when the afternoon newspaper appeared, he thought as he waited. The police had arranged to have the boy's picture and name at the bottom of the front page. Obviously the boy had relatives, classmates, teachers, neighbors. Yes, the chances were excellent that the whole thing would come to a head this afternoon.

Marilyn checked the grandfather clock near the living-room archway: 1:30. The antique dealer, a Mr. Hardin, of Hardin and Hardin, Antiques, was due in an hour. With his truck. She wondered if she should tidy things up for him—dust here and there, vacuum, wash down the walls where Greg had left his dirty little fingerprints. Goddamnit, she'd be forever liberating the house from Greg and Brett's corruptive, lingering, nasty presence. Forever! She'd need new sheets, to begin with, and new pillowcases. And she'd need new toilet fixtures, too. And new mattresses, new quilts, new flatware . . . Christ, was there anything they hadn't touched, anything at all left that she wouldn't have to change, make right, clean, cover over? Anything?

Only the room, she realized.

Her room.

She suddenly cocked her head toward the stairway. Were those really the soft cries of a child she was hearing? She listened. The sounds stopped abruptly, and she decided it had probably come from outside—a pigeon under the eaves, some kids passing by, a breeze moving around the house. It wouldn't be the first time, she reminded herself, that the house had made noises of its own.

The phone rang. She snapped her gaze toward it, quickly angered by the intrusion. She went to it.

"Yes?" She hoped her tone carried her annoyance.

"Mrs. Courtney?"

"Yes."

"This is George Hardin; we spoke a short while ago."

"What is it, Mr. Hardin?"

"If it's convenient, Mrs. Courtney, I'd like to come over immediately. You see, another client called to change his appointment——"

"It's fine with me, Mr. Hardin."

"Good. I'll see you in ten or fifteen minutes?"

"Yes. I'll be waiting, Mr. Hardin. Good-bye."

She went to the kitchen, opened a closet door, got out dust rags, a mop, a broom, floor wax, lemon-oil furniture polish. Soon her arms were so burdened that she dropped the can of furniture polish. She swore, and kicked it toward the hallway.

* * *

Christine wished Tim had stayed home. It was difficult being alone in the house today, uncomfortable—
as if something had taken Tim's place when he left and
was following her from room to room. Not a malevolent something. It might even be herself that followed
her, that lingered at each window she passed and in
every doorway, counseling *Slow down*—her rational
self berating her for the turmoil she had allowed to
grow inside her, her rational self punishing her for
holding onto the dream momentarily, then letting it
go. Because that was the way small children behaved.

She remembered, with almost frantic fondness, the
story Becky Foster had told her about the Cornhill
ghosts: "Each house has one. Yours is of a young
woman killed when the roof of this house collapsed."
She longed for just such a ghost—for some classic, un-
seen, archetypal thing she could blame her fears on.

But there was no ghost. Only her fears, and her
turmoil, and something inside slowly tearing her apart.
It had spent the last nine months at it, and its growth
had produced only unanswerable questions:

Why (the first question) had she demanded that Tim
buy *this* house? Even restored it was ugly, without
charm, claustrophobic.

And why (the second question) had she so willingly
accepted Becky Foster's offer of friendship and then,
without reason, rejected it, as if that friendship had
suddenly become an unnecessary burden?

And why in God's name had she opened her arms
to Marilyn Courtney, accepted her gifts and confi-
dences as if hungry for the details of her life, for a live
sketch of her psyche?

And why the dreams, the exhaustion, the glimpses
into her own, blank future?

"Christ!"

She found herself in the small foyer, facing Jimmy
Wheeler's portrait. And the thing following her about
the house—not her rational self at all, she realized,

but . . . desperation? helplessness? Jesus, how did she define it?—pulled her away from the portrait. It was only a painting now—something dead and useless.

Marilyn gestured stiffly at the three T-shirted men standing behind Mr. Hardin: "Please tell them to wait outside, Mr. Hardin."

Hardin, a short, thin man in his late sixties, nodded, and the men stepped back from the door. "May I come in, Mrs. Courtney?"

"Of course." She held her arm out toward the inside of the house.

Hardin stepped in and glanced about. He adjusted his wire-rimmed glasses on his nose, harumphed: "You have a very large house, Mrs. Courtney. You said on the telephone that you wish to sell everything?"

"Almost everything, Mr. Hardin. All except for one room's worth."

He nodded at a pecan settee near the entranceway. "Now, *that's* a nice item, Mrs. Courtney."

Marilyn said nothing: Hardin's tone said he wanted to haggle about price, and she was not in the mood for haggling.

Chapter 35

Roger Peterson looked up at the man in the doorway. The man said, "There was no one at the desk; I guess it's past her quitting time, right?" He indicated the receptionist's desk, behind him. "So I came in. Are you Mr. Peterson?"

"I am. And you are——"

"Brett Courtney." He paused briefly. "You've got my son."

Peterson stood slowly and nodded at the chair opposite his desk. He used his most officious tone: "Please sit down, Mr. Courtney. I have some questions I'd like to ask you."

"Tell me first how Greg is. They wouldn't tell me a thing at the hospital. They sent me here."

"He's listed as satisfactory now."

Brett lowered his head. "Thank God."

"For a while it was pretty much anyone's guess. But he'll pull through. I assume, Mr. Courtney, that you saw the boy's picture in the newspaper."

"Yes."

"Could you tell me why neither you nor your wife came forward till now?"

"My wife and I are separated, Mr. Peterson. Not legally—not yet, anyway." He paused: Did Peterson believe him? He had rehearsed the whole thing a dozen times on the way over. "I've been living at the Alexander Street Apartments for the past week or so." And that was true enough, if Peterson wanted to check,

234

though Brett couldn't remember going back there. After escaping the attic, he had been fog-bound for at least a day. "Greg and I, that is."

"Do you think you could tell me how your son happened to turn up on the steps of the Sibley Building?"

"Yes. I have an office there. He knew that. I can only guess he had another of his nightmares——"

"Nightmares?"

"He's plagued by them, Mr. Peterson. He's under psychiatric care, as a matter of fact." Also true. "And sometimes these nightmares frighten him so badly that he panics. That's apparently what he did last night. He panicked."

Peterson looked skeptical, Brett thought, but not disbelieving. This was, after all, the best way to go. Marilyn had obviously grown tired of Greg and thrown him out, frightened him away. Eventually—when he had Greg with him—Brett could deal with Marilyn in his own way, on his own terms. If he told the truth now, there would be so many difficult questions, and so many clumsy answers. Besides, it was possible—perhaps even likely—that, in the end, Marilyn could regain custody, could turn the tables and somehow prove that Brett was negligent, culpable. It would be, after all, one on one—his word against hers.

"I take it, Mr. Courtney, that you left Greg alone last night?"

"Yes, I'm afraid I did. Marilyn and I had started doing that from time to time about six months ago. He's usually quite a responsible child——"

"Mr. Courtney, he's only, what—eight, nine years old?"

"Nine, actually. He'll be ten in June. Marilyn and I felt it was time——"

"Marilyn's your wife?"

"Yes."

"Could I have her address, please? For the records."

"I'm afraid I don't know it, Mr. Peterson. I know she's living somewhere in Buffalo and using her maiden name." Yes, that was a good touch.

"And what is her maiden name, please?"

"King. K-I-N-G."

Peterson wrote the name on a form of some kind. He looked up. "Could you tell me where you were last night? Again, just for the record."

"I was in a motel, in Honeoye. That's about forty miles south of here. I had planned to come home about midnight, you see, but there was a storm——"

"Did you try to call your son? Or maybe a neighbor? This is a very serious thing we're dealing with here, Mr. Courtney. Leaving a nine-year-old alone overnight is extremely poor judgment, don't you think?"

"Yes, I do." Brett would take the lecture. He thought he actually deserved it, considering his years of neglect toward Greg. "And it won't happen again, Mr. Peterson."

Peterson sighed; it had been a long day, and this man seemed sincere enough. "The police will probably have a few questions, Mr. Courtney. This is a possible child-abuse case, you understand; that's why I'm handling it. I don't believe I'll recommend that the D.A. file charges; however, I do hope you'll be a bit more careful in the future. Your boy came this close"—he snapped his fingers—"to dying. Do you realize that, Mr. Courtney?"

"Yes, yes, I realize that." Brett lowered his head, as if in supplication.

"I hope you do, Mr. Courtney. I really hope you do." He wrote furiously on a sheet of memo paper, handed it to Brett. "Give this to the doctor in charge of your son's case; he'll let you in to see him. I'll call ahead to verify it."

Brett stood, thrust out his hand. Peterson took it.

"Thank you, sir." Brett was genuinely pleased. "Thank you very much."

Marilyn stared hard at the attic door. Nothing, she told herself; nothing was behind it. The past was behind it. And the past was dead. Buried. Decayed.

The itch was on her wrists again. And again she felt it beneath her fingernails as the blood started. She sucked hungrily at the blood. She turned, ran. She stopped.

Only the floor-standing mirror remained, and the high-backed red leather chair, so old and sturdy; the large, exquisitely detailed oriental rug; the robin's-egg-blue Haviland washbasin; the little black-walnut table. Greg and Brett had never come to this room. Never. Not in ten years. They had never had reason. The house was big enough. Even she had all but forgotten about it after the first couple years. It was a big, airy room—the biggest and airiest in the house. And now it was the last vestige of what she had worked so hard to build, what Greg and Brett had defiled and thus destroyed.

She studied herself in the mirror and decided she liked what she saw very much. She was the Grande Dame, Mistress of the House, who had spurned a thousand suitors in favor of more noble pastimes. Heads hung bloodless from tall poles for her sake. Men waged wars for her sake:

She was Mistress of the House.

She laughed suddenly, softly. This was a pleasant game. She moved her hands slowly over her breasts, her stomach; she lifted her chin.

"Marilyn?" she heard. "Marilyn, are you here?"

Emptied, Brett thought incredulously. *The goddamned house has been fucking emptied!*

"Some of these items, as I've said, are really very nice, Mrs. Courtney."

"All of these items are priceless, Mr. Hardin, and you know it. But I didn't call you here to haggle over price. I called you here because all of this stuff has to go. As quickly as possible."

"Marilyn?" Brett waited a moment, fascinated by the way her name caromed off the walls of the house. It was such a . . . terminal sound. "Marilyn, are you here?" He waited again. Still nothing. "My God," he murmured. He hadn't expected this. If she loved anything in this world, it was her house and her houseful of furniture. They were her identity.

He passed through the living room, into the hallway. He started for the stairs.

"It's . . . three-thirty now, Mrs. Courtney, and I've yet to appraise several roomsful of furniture. This is not a process that can be rushed; I'm sure you realize that."

"This is a process that must be rushed, Mr. Hardin. The price you've given me is fair; I accept it. As for what's left—take it; it's yours."

"Mrs. Courtney, I couldn't——"

"I'm not asking you; I'm telling you. I want this house empty by tomorrow morning."

Brett mounted the stairs slowly. The empty house intrigued him. It was as if he was seeing it for the first time. He knew why: Marilyn had been exorcized from it. She had exorcized herself. Now it was just a big, empty house. Ugly and sterile. Even the memories had been exorcized.

He stopped halfway up the stairs. "Marilyn?" he called, loudly. He grinned at the way the name came back at him a half-dozen times, each time softer, until it was just a tinny whisper, an almost mechanical thing. It made Brett happy. "Marilyn," he called again, even louder; but he expected no response. He got none.

"We can take many of these items now, Mrs. Courtney, if that is your wish. And later in the week——"

"Perhaps I didn't make myself clear, Mr. Hardin. Or perhaps I called the wrong man. All of this stuff has to be out of here by tomorrow morning. All of it. If you and your men are not up to it . . ."

"Mrs. Courtney, do you realize the extra expense involved? The extra manpower? I do have another truck, but——"

"Damn your expense, Mr. Hardin, and damn you! If it's that freakin' important, deduct it from the price you quoted!"

Brett turned, descended the stairs, and crossed to the door. He wondered only briefly where Marilyn had gone. She had no relatives in the city; her nearest relatives were in Syracuse, so perhaps she had gone there. And perhaps she had had the furniture stored, or shipped. Perhaps she had sold it. Brett didn't care very much. After a while, he thought, he'd put the house on the market. Someone would buy it, eventually. Someone like Marilyn. And they'd fill it with antiques, and it would once again come to life. He chuckled at that.

He opened the front door, glanced back. All the memories were gone from this place now. Most of them were bad, so to hell with them. He had Greg, and Greg was all that mattered. He only felt sorry that he was so long in realizing it.

"We'll do our best, Mrs. Courtney, but I can't promise——"

"You can promise, Mr. Hardin, and you will; otherwise I'll call someone else. Do you want me to call someone else?"

"No, Mrs. Courtney."

Tim realized he was trembling. He forced himself to steady the receiver in his hand: "Dr. Tichell?"

"I got your message, Mr. Bennet. I would have called back sooner, but I was unavoidably detained. What seems to be the problem?"

"It's Christine, Doctor. She's sick—fever, chills; her

fever seems to be awfully high." Tim felt himself breaking down. He took a deep breath, held it a moment.

"Yes, Mr. Bennet, go on."

"I can't seem to wake her, Doctor."

"How long has she been unconscious?"

"An hour and a half, two hours . . . longer, maybe.
I got home and found her this way."

"Are you still at your Cornhill address, Mr. Bennet?"

"Yes, we are. Should I——"

"I'll be there within fifteen minutes. Try and keep
her fever down, if possible—wet towels, ice packs. I'll
be there shortly."

Chapter 36

Surely the evening, and now sunrise, had cleansed the house of his spirit. Surely it was hers now. Hers alone. He had been looking for her; he hadn't found her (he didn't know about this room), so he had gone away. Forever.

Marilyn closed her hand over the doorknob, turned it, opened the door an inch. She peered out.

Morning sunlight through the stained-glass window at the end of the hall cast patches of blue and red and yellow on the bare wood floor. The rest of the hallway was in semidarkness, as if the three doors along its length were open and one candle burned in each room. It was the kind of darkness that spoke softly—but with certainty—of abandonment.

The house was empty; Marilyn knew it.

She opened her door wide, held it open with her left hand. A wide, pleased smile spread over her face.

It had been so simple. Really so simple.

She would call the painters today. And Ethan Allen Furniture. They'd send a representative over, and she and the representative would spend long, happy hours discussing the house's new decor. It would be a marvelous day.

Maybe Christine could help her. Christine was, after all, an artist, and interior decoration was a form of art. She had certainly made her own little house quite presentable.

Marilyn moved quickly, jauntily, to the staircase,

started down. She stopped, thought: She would tell the representative that nothing contemporary or Mediterranean or avant-garde would be allowed. Only authentic period pieces that oozed strength and solidity; only pieces like that could adequately mirror her own personality.

It would be a marvelous day.

And the painters . . . Pastels, of course, were out. Only firm colors—deep greens and dark blues. White, of course, would have its place, but mainly to provide contrast for the cherrywood molding in the parlor and the dining room.

She'd have the kitchen completely refurbished, take out the stove and the refrigerator-freezer and the dishwasher. It was all so modern, so lifeless, so mortal. Marilyn laughed at that. Lifeless and mortal. Her giddiness—she suddenly felt much younger—was producing nonsense.

She heard herself giggle. She put her hand to her mouth. "Uh-oh," she said; she liked the way it felt in her chest, the buoyancy of it, the freedom of it. "Uh-oh," she repeated. And heard someone call her name.

"Mith King?" she heard.

She glanced about, confused.

"Mith King?" she heard again.

"Who's there?" She looked toward the top of the stairs. She saw nothing. "Who is it?" she said.

"It's me, Marilyn," she heard.

She looked toward the bottom of the stairs. The voice was suddenly familiar.

"Hello, Marilyn. Your house is quite empty."

Marilyn blinked twice, rapidly. "Christine? How'd you get in?"

"You had that ramp built for me, don't you remember? And you gave me a key."

"I gave you no key."

"Oh, but you did, Marilyn. See?" She reached into

the folds of the checkered blanket wrapped around her legs and withdrew a huge iron key. It could not possibly have worked the lock to Marilyn's front door— seemed more like the key to some medieval castle. "Here it is." She held it out; it gleamed dully. "You must have forgotten, Marilyn. You gave it to me several days ago. You said we were like sisters, so I should have a key to your house. Do you really think we're like sisters, Marilyn?"

Marilyn said nothing.

"I had no real sisters, Marilyn. Or brothers. I was an only child. Did I ever tell you that?"

"No, you didn't." Marilyn's voice was a choked monotone.

"An only child, yes. And quite spoiled, my parents tell me. Most only children are spoiled, I hear. Not enough discipline. Everybody's got to get whacked around once in a while, isn't that right, Marilyn?"

"I . . . don't know."

"I can't hear you, Marilyn. Why are you whispering? Are you afraid of something?"

"No."

"No? But you really should be. If I were you, I'd be scared to death. I'd be petrified!"

"Who *are* you?"

"I'm your neighbor, Christine Bennet. And we go back a long way, you and I. A long, long way."

Marilyn started backing up the stairs very slowly. "I would like you to . . . to go away now, Christine."

"And leave you alone? That wouldn't be neighborly, Marilyn. I'll leave, yes. Right away. But I can't leave you alone."

Marilyn turned.

She saw the 9-iron first.

"Certainly not alone, Marilyn."

And Brett's hand resting on the grip. And his wide, white grin. He said nothing.

"I know what it's like to be alone, Marilyn. You left me alone, once. Do you remember?"

Marilyn felt her stomach turn over. Her gaze riveted on the deep, dark-blue gash at the side of Brett's head, close to his ear. His grin increased.

"*They* will be here with you, Marilyn."

And Greg appeared, his eyes wide and round and staring, his skin the color of eggshells; he had a stark look of surprise and weariness about him. "Mommy," he said, and Marilyn had a quick picture of herself reaching behind him and winding him up, or pulling his string. "Mommy," he repeated.

"They will *always* be with you, Marilyn."

Marilyn's head snapped from right to left. "No," she murmured. She stumbled past her husband and her son, up the stairs. On the landing she turned left. She looked back.

Greg and Brett were slowly turning to follow.

Dr. Tichell's tone was apologetic: "Mr. Bennet, I must be truthful with you; I cannot yet adequately diagnose your wife's condition. It seems very much like a severe flu, but, even in severe cases, we rarely encounter fevers as high as hers, except in children. And when we do, the fever almost always responds to medication." He paused. "There is," he continued, "another possibility—toxic-shock syndrome. It's something relatively new, like Legionnaire's disease."

"Legionnaire's disease?" Tim was suddenly close to panic.

Tichell explained hurriedly, "Only in the respect that it *is* new, Mr. Bennet, something not encountered widely until a few years ago. Christine's symptoms are almost classic——"

"Can you treat it?"

"Yes, we can, if it *is* toxic-shock syndrome. It's actually a staph infection, you see."

"Dr. Tichell"—he was close to panic again—"will she live, for Christ's sake?"

Tichell put his hand comfortingly on Tim's shoulder. "I've been your wife's doctor for a long time, Mr. Bennet, almost fifteen years. And I've gotten to know her quite well—especially from a medical standpoint. She's a very very strong woman, and I think she has a strong will to live."

Tim lowered his head; Tichell could say no more than that, he realized.

The paging system squawked: "Dr. Tichell to Intensive Care . . . Dr. Tichell to Intensive Care . . ."

Tichell stood abruptly. Tim stood.

"No," Tichell said. "You'll have to stay here, Mr. Bennet. Trust me."

Tim looked helplessly at him. "But——"

"Trust me, Mr. Bennet," Tichell repeated. He left the waiting room quickly.

Marilyn watched the closed door move inward slightly, heard the dull thudding noises from the other side. She put her hand to her mouth, curled her fingers up. "Don't," she whispered. "Please!" She reached out very quickly, turned the key in the lock, withdrew the key. She backed up a step, hesitated, took another step, and another. "Don't!" She felt the back of her foot connect with something. She glanced around, saw the black-walnut table fall, watched the robin's-egg-blue washbasin fall with it, watched it hit the floor and shatter into a dozen large pieces. "Please," she whispered.

"Marilyn," she heard. It was Brett's voice—low, insistent, a little off-key, as if he wanted to tell her some grotesque joke.

"Mommy." Greg's voice—a high-pitched, brittle, mechanical screech. *I want!* it said. *I want, I want, I want!*

Marilyn screamed, "Go away! Go away from my house!"

The door moved inward.

The dull thudding noises continued.

Tichell had no expression. Tim stood, waited for him to cross the room, and realized, suddenly, *Jesus, the man is wearing a poker face—something's happened!* "She's dead, isn't she," Tim called. "My wife is dead!"

Tichell covered the remaining few feet quickly. He helped Tim into a chair. "No," he said. "No, Mr. Bennet. Her fever has risen slightly, that's all. A degree. Not even a degree."

"You mean you can't . . . you can't bring it back down?"

"We are doing what we can, Mr. Bennet. What happens from this point is as much up to Christine as it is up to anyone. I told you before, she has a strong will to live——"

"May I . . . see her?"

The doctor thought a moment. "You can look in on her, yes." Tim was immediately suspicious of the concession. Was the doctor allowing him one last look? "But please remember," Tichell continued, "that she may not recognize you. She slips in and out of consciousness. And she's been babbling."

"Babbling?"

"It's not uncommon in cases of high fever, Mr. Bennet."

"Has she been calling for me? Is that what she's been saying—my name?"

"From time to time, yes, Mr. Bennet. She has said your name several times." He stood. "I'll take you to her."

Tim stood and followed him to Intensive Care.

He didn't like what he saw. The hospital's efforts to keep Christine alive had reduced her to something half-machine, half-human.

"I should have warned you about all this; I'm sorry," Tichell said. "But without it, Christine would——"

"I understand, Doctor."

"Yes, I believe you do." Tichell addressed the nurse by Christine's bedside: "Has her fever stabilized?"

"It's holding at a hundred and five point five, Doctor. There's been no change in the last fifteen minutes."

Tim nodded grimly at the heart monitor above the bed; it was beeping steadily, rhythmically. "Can't you turn that thing down or something?"

"I'm afraid that wouldn't——" Tichell began.

And Christine interrupted: "Mith King?"

Tim's mouth dropped open. He looked helplessly from Tichell to the nurse to Tichell; his gaze steadied on Christine. "My God," he said. "My God, what was that? That wasn't even her voice. My God." It had been the voice of a child—a very small child. "Dr. Tichell, please——"

"Mith King? I'm thorry, Mith King."

"It's a regression of sorts, Mr. Bennet."

"A regression? To what? I don't understand."

"To her childhood—her early childhood, I'd guess."

"Thirsty, Mith King. Cold, Mith King."

"Christ!" Tim muttered.

"Apparently she's reliving the time before her accident —the accident that paralyzed her. Before I brought you in here, she made some oblique, but unmistakable, references to walking. The accident itself was, of course, a traumatic time for her, an *extremely* traumatic time for her, and it has——"

"My dolly, *my* dolly!"

"It has stayed with her, Mr. Bennet—the essence of it, the flavor of it."

"I'm thorry, Mith King."

Tichell said, "I don't know who this 'Miss King' was, but it's obvious that Christine is using her now as a kind of handhold to the past. And it's possible that the child you're listening to—locked up inside Christine all these years—is replaying events in an attempt to correct them, in an attempt to change history, so to speak." Tichell paused, pursed his lips. He shook his head slowly. "And it's possible, Mr. Bennet, that I don't know what the hell I'm talking about. I must be truthful with you——"

"Dr. Tichell?" It was the nurse.

"Yes?"

"Her fever's dropped. It's a hundred and four point nine now."

Tim smiled nervously. "That's good, isn't it?"

"It might be," Tichell said. "You'll have to leave now."

"But——"

"Please. For her sake."

Tim left reluctantly.

Marilyn held her breath. Listened. It had all stopped so abruptly. The house was quiet now; she could hear only an early spring rain pinging against the room's three large windows, and something—a mouse?—scurrying about inside the walls. Quiet sounds.

She stared blankly at the broken washbasin. It had been such a treasure, so beautiful, so frail, so very, very old, as old as the house itself, older maybe——

"Brett?" She said the name tentatively, cautiously. "Brett, are you there?" In fear he would answer, she hurried on: "Brett, are you there? Go away now. You have no place here. This is my house. You have the attic. Take the attic. Both of you." She moved slowly toward the door. "I'm sorry I hurt you, either of you; I *am* sorry." She put her hand on the knob, turned it. "I'm coming out now and I don't want to see you there. I don't." As she opened the door, she closed her eyes tightly. "Go away now," she said, her voice low and pleading. She opened her eyes. She saw the stained-glass window at the opposite end of the hall. It was dull now; it cast no colorful pattern on the wood floor. Marilyn kept her eyes on it; she felt a tear slide down her cheek.

"Dr. Tichell, her fever's rising—a hundred and five."
"Oh, good Christ. I want more ice packs."
"A hundred and five point three."
"This is absolutely unbelievable."
"Mith King?"

The hands were Brett's; Marilyn knew it immediately. They touched, caressed, probed as if she were naked.

Her body stiffened under those hands; her eyes shut. She felt the hands suddenly tugging at her, heard Brett's voice:

"Come, Marilyn. Away from that room."

"Doctor, her fever's at a hundred and six."
"Get an ice bath ready, nurse."
"Yes, sir."
"We can't let this fever go any higher."

Marilyn snapped her eyes open. She thought at first that it was the stained-glass window she was seeing, its dull blues and reds and yellows fused at the edges. And then she saw that the colors had form, substance, topography—here, what had been a nose; there, the places where eyes should be; and below, the dark mouth, opened as if in an endless yawn. The yawn narrowed and expanded rapidly, like the sucking motion of a fish. Words came from it: "Come away from that room, Marilyn. Come away from that room."

And Marilyn realized instantly where safety lay.

She struggled desperately against Brett's strong grip.

* * *

"A hundred and six point five, Doctor."

"Where is that damned ice bath? This woman has only moments to live!"

Marilyn's gaze fell slowly, disbelievingly, down the length of the thing tugging at her, pleading with her, touching her. She lurched away from it, stepped to the side of it.

And saw her son at the end of the hallway.

He was waving, smiling, telling her in his gestures, *Come here!*

One word—"Nooooo!"—escaped her, but, in its pitch and volume, it was unintelligible.

Like an automaton, she turned. And saw the open door to her room. The broken washbasin. The windows, and the soft, steady rain hugging them. The old, sturdy chair.

Safety. Security. Peace, and quiet.

She stumbled through the open door, felt a hand at the back of her housedress. "Noooooo!" she repeated, and wrenched free of it.

She turned again, threw her weight against the door, fumbled for the key—"Oh, God! Oh, God!"—found it, shoved it into the lock, turned it.

And crumpled, smiling, to the floor.

She was safe. *Here* she was safe.

This was her room.

A big, beautiful, airy room.

"Doctor, her fever's down to a hundred and five."

"Blood pressure?"

"Increasing. Heart rhythm normalizing."

"I don't understand any of this."

"A hundred and four now."

"I really do not——"

"A hundred and three, Doctor. She appears to be regaining consciousness."

"Christine? Christine, can you hear me?"

"A hundred and two."

"Christine?"

"Dr. Tichell?"

"Yes, Christine. You're in the hospital. You were quite ill, but——"

"Why? Why am I in the hospital?"

"You were sick, Christine. You had us a little worried, as a matter of fact."

"Dr. Tichell, where's Tim? Where's my husband?"

"I'll bring him to you shortly, Christine. Right now, I think you've got to rest a while."

Christine's eyes closed slowly, and she sighed. "Yes," she said. "I do feel a little weary. I feel like I've run ten miles." She smiled. "Tell Tim I love him very much. Tell him I'm all right, now."

She was asleep.

Her room. Let them wait outside. Let them! If they could wait forever, so could she.

And let them have the house. Let them corrupt it, dirty it, leave their droppings all around.

Let them wander back to that door. And wait there forever.

She'd beat them.

It didn't matter.

She would beat them!

Chapter 37

Four weeks later

Sonny Norton was happy the winter was ending. Spring brought the people out of their houses—the children especially, and they were fun to watch. He thought, suddenly, that that is what he might do this year: just watch. Because maybe he was getting a little old to be playing with the children. A little old, and a little big, and a little clumsy. Things changed. He had changed.

In the room, the woman in the big, comfortable chair was beginning to close in on herself, like an old jack-o'-lantern. In the first few days here she had moved haltingly back and forth, back and forth, from the door to the chair to the window and back to the door, at one moment convinced that the things on the other side of the door had gone, and, at the next, equally convinced that the things waited for her very patiently. Very quietly. Because they had an eternity to wait. And nothing else to do.

The woman in the chair couldn't know the truth—that her husband and her son had started a new life together, that, in time, it would be a good and happy life. Despite the memories. The woman in the chair believed what she had seen. And felt. Because, like all of us, she was a slave to her senses. The things beyond

the door were real because they had called to her,
touched her, driven her here, into this big, airy room.
And now—there was no doubt; it was an absolute and
awful certainty—they waited for her to come out.

But, she told herself (as she had told herself a hundred times), she would beat them.

Sonny Norton shoved his hands into his pockets. He
wondered if he was sad about the pictures going away.
He had never understood them, and sometimes they
frightened him. There were many things he did not understand, and many things that frightened him—babies,
for instance, and the big, noisy street-cleaning machines,
and thunderstorms. But they were all things he had to
live with, and sometimes he enjoyed them.

"Hi," he heard. He looked up.

The boy was smiling warmly; he had a wet snowball
in his bare hands.

Sonny said, "Better put that in the 'frigerator or
it'll melt."

"Naw," the boy said, "it won't melt; it's too cold."
He heaved the snowball at a lamppost, missed it, bent
over, scooped up some more snow, packed it hard. He
hefted the finished snowball and looked pleased. "See
ya," he said, waving slightly, and ran off.

Sonny watched until the boy rounded the corner onto
Aberdeen Street; then he turned and started walking
again.

The woman in the chair had sensed the approach of
death several days before, as if it were a train just
beyond the horizon and she could do nothing but sit
and wait for it. That is when she had started babbling.
"Thank God for the space between us, Brett," she said,
over and over again, like a windup doll. "Thank God
for the space between us, Brett." Eventually, her mouth

stopped working and she began repeating the words mentally. It was an attempt to shut out the images that had been assaulting her since her second day here. Images of the things on the other side of the door. Images of Christine and of the child Christine had been, and of the vengeance that child had taken, at last. "Thank God for the space between us, Brett."

On the sixteenth day, these words came back to her and she wanted, needed to cry, but couldn't: "They will *always* be with you, Marilyn."

The woman in the big, comfortable chair in the big, airy room silently repeated the words again and again: "They will *always* be with you, Marilyn." Because there was sense in the words, reason in the words—a reason for her to be in the room. To be dying in it.

On the twenty-eighth day, at a little past 3:00 P.M., these words—as if from an ancient wax cylinder—came from the woman, very quickly, on a long and shuddering exhale: "And no no I'm not sorry not freakin' sorry to you Christine, go to hell, or to anyone." And her lungs and heart stopped, and she thought, incredulously, *This is death? This is death? Big deal! All those stupid scare stories, shit on 'em, shit on 'em. Oh, Jesus! Oh, Jesus! I want to live. Jesus, I want to live! I want——"*

In front of the Bennet house, Sonny Norton stopped once more. The house was empty, his sister had told him—though she hadn't needed to; he could feel that it was empty. The young couple had moved out. A pity, his sister said—they seemed to fit so nicely in Cornhill. Sonny knew better.

He turned his head and studied the Courtney house a long while. He saw a curtain move slightly in one of the second-floor windows. Only the wind, he supposed. It was an empty house. As empty as death. He had nothing to fear from an empty house.

He bent over, scooped up some snow, packed it hard. He hefted the snowball. Maybe what he'd do when he got home was put it in the refrigerator. Maybe that's what he'd do. Then he could save a little bit of this winter forever.

PLAYBOY NOVELS OF
HORROR AND THE OCCULT
ABSOLUTELY
CHILLING